Herman Charles
Bosman

A BEKKERSDAL
MARATHON

Scrawny Goat Books

Herman Charles Bosman

A BEKKERSDAL MARATHON

Scrawny Goat Books
152 City Road
London, EC1V 2PD
United Kingdom

scrawnygoatbooks.com

ISBN 978-1-64764-437-6

CONTENTS

A BEKKERSDAL MARATHON

AT Naudé, who had a wireless set, came into Jurie Steyn's voorkamer, where we were sitting waiting for the Government lorry from Bekkersdal, and gave us the latest news. He said that the newest thing in Europe was that young people there were going in for non-stop dancing. It was called marathon dancing, At Naudé told us, and those young people were trying to break the record for who could remain on their feet longest, dancing.

We listened for a while to what At Naudé had to say, and then we suddenly remembered a marathon event that had taken place in the little dorp of Bekkersdal — almost in our midst, you could say. What was more, there were quite a number of us sitting in Jurie Steyn's post office who had actually taken part in that non-stop affair, and without knowing that we were breaking records, and without expecting any sort of a prize for it, either.

We discussed that affair at considerable length and from all angles, and we were still talking about it when the lorry came. And we agreed that it had been in several respects an unusual occurrence. We also agreed that it was questionable whether we could have carried off things so successfully that day if it had not been for Billy Robertse.

You see, our organist at Bekkersdal was Billy Robertse. He had once been a sailor and had come to the bushveld some years before, travelling on foot. His belongings, fastened in a red handkerchief, were slung over his shoulder on a stick. Billy Robertse was journeying in that fashion for the sake of his health. He suffered from an unfortunate complaint for which he had at regular intervals to drink something out of a black bottle that he always carried handy in his jacket-pocket.

Billy Robertse would even keep that bottle beside him in the organist's gallery in case of a sudden attack. And if the hymn the

1

predikant gave out had many verses, you could be sure that about half-way through Billy Robertse would bring the bottle up to his mouth, leaning sideways towards what was in it. And he would put several extra twirls into the second part of the hymn.

When he first applied for the position of organist in the Bekkersdal church, Billy Robertse told the meeting of deacons that he had learnt to play the organ in a cathedral in Northern Europe. Several deacons felt, then, that they could not favour his application. They said that the cathedral sounded too Papist, the way Billy Robertse described it, with a dome 300 ft. high and with marble apostles.

But it was lucky for Billy Robertse that he was able to mention, at the following combined meeting of elders and deacons, that he had also played the piano in a South American dance hall, of which the manager had been a Presbyterian. He asked the meeting to overlook his unfortunate past, saying that he had had a hard life, and anybody could make mistakes. In any case, he had never cared much for the Romish atmosphere of the cathedral, he said, and had been happier in the dance hall.

In the end, Billy Robertse got the appointment. But in his sermons for several Sundays after that the predikant, Dominee Welthagen, had spoken very strongly against the evils of dance halls. He described those places of awful sin in such burning words that at least one young man went to see Billy Robertse, privately, with a view to taking lessons in playing the piano.

But Billy Robertse was a good musician. And he took a deep interest in his work. And he said that when he sat down on the organist's stool behind the pulpit, and his fingers were flying over the keyboards, and he was pulling out the stops, and his feet were pressing down the notes that sent the deep bass tones through the pipes — then he felt that he could play all day, he said.

I don't suppose he guessed that he would one day be put to the test, however.

It all happened through Dominee Welthagen one Sunday morning going into a trance in the pulpit. And we did not realise that he was in a trance. It was an illness that overtook him in a strange and sudden fashion.

At each service the predikant, after reading a passage from the Bible, would lean forward with his hand on the pulpit rail and give out the number of the hymn we had to sing. For years his manner of conducting the service had been exactly the same. He would say, for instance: "We will now sing Psalm 82, verses 1 to 4." Then he would allow his head to sink forward on to his chest and he would remain rigid, as though in prayer, until the last notes of the hymn died away in the church.

Now, on that particular morning, just after he had announced the number of the psalm, without mentioning what verses, Dominee Welthagen again took a firm grip on the pulpit rail and allowed his head to sink forward on to his breast. We did not realise that he had fallen into a trance of a peculiar character that kept his body standing upright while his mind was a blank. We learnt that only later.

In the meantime, while the organ was playing over the opening bars, we began to realise that Dominee Welthagen had not indicated how many verses we had to sing. But he would discover his mistake, we thought, after we had been singing for a few minutes.

All the same, one or two of the younger members of the congregation did titter, slightly, when they took up their hymn-books. For Dominee Welthagen had given out Psalm 119. And everybody knows that Psalm 119 has 176 verses.

This was a church service that will never be forgotten in Bekkersdal.

We sang the first verse and then the second and then the third. When we got to about the sixth verse and the minister still gave no sign that it would be the last, we assumed that he wished us to sing the first eight verses. For, if you open your hymn-book, you'll see that Psalm 119 is divided into sets of eight verses, each ending with the word "Pause".

We ended the last notes of verse eight with more than an ordinary number of turns and twirls, confident that at any moment Dominee Welthagen would raise his head and let us know that we could sing "Amen".

It was when the organ started up very slowly and solemnly with the music for verse nine that a real feeling of disquiet overcame the congregation. But, of course, we gave no sign of what went on in our minds. We held Dominee Welthagen in too much veneration.

Nevertheless, I would rather not say too much about our feelings, when verse followed verse and Pouse succeeded Pouse, and still Dominee Welthagen made no sign that we had sung long enough, or that there was anything unusual in what he was demanding of us.

After they had recovered from their first surprise, the members of the church council conducted themselves in a most exemplary manner. Elders and deacons tiptoed up and down the aisles, whispering words of reassurance to such members of the congregation, men as well as women, who gave signs of wanting to panic.

At one stage it looked as though we were going to have trouble from the organist. That was when Billy Robertse, at the end of the 34th verse, held up his black bottle and signalled quietly to the elders to indicate that his medicine was finished. At the end of the 35th verse he made signals of a less quiet character, and again at the end of the 36th verse. That was when Elder Landsman tiptoed out of the church and went round to the Konsistorie, where the Nagmaal wine was kept. When Elder Landsman came back into the church, he had a long black bottle half hidden under his manel. He took the bottle up to the organist's gallery, still walking on tiptoe.

At verse 61 there was almost a breakdown. That was when a message came from the back of the organ, where Koster Claassen and the assistant verger, whose task it was to turn the handle that kept the organ supplied with wind, were in a state near to exhaustion. So, it was Deacon Cronje's turn to go tiptoeing out of the church. Deacon Cronje was head warder at the local goal. When he came back it was with three burly Native convicts in striped jerseys, who also went through the church on tiptoe. They arrived just in time to take over the handle from Koster Claassen and the assistant verger.

At verse 98 the organist again started making signals about his medicine. Once more, Elder Landsman went round to the konsistorie. This time he was accompanied by another elder and a deacon, and they stayed away somewhat longer than the time when Elder Landsman had gone on his own. On their return the deacon bumped into a small hymn-book table at the back of the church. Perhaps it was because the deacon was a fat, red-faced man, and not used to tiptoeing.

At verse 124 the organist signalled again, and the same three members of the church council filed out to the konsistorie, the deacon walking in front this time.

It was about then that the pastor of the Full Gospel Apostolic Faith Church, about whom Dominee Welthagen had in the past used almost as strong language as about the Pope, came up to the front gate of the church to see what was afoot. He lived near our church and, having heard the same hymn-tune being played over and over for about eight hours, he was a very amazed man. Then he saw the door of the konsistorie open, and two elders and a deacon coming out, walking on tiptoe — they having apparently forgotten that they were not in church, then. When the pastor saw one of the elders hiding a black bottle under his manel, a look of understanding came over his features. The pastor walked off, shaking his head.

At verse 152 the organist signalled again. This time Elder Landsman and the other elder went out alone. The deacon stayed behind in the deacon's bench, apparently in deep thought. The organist signalled again, for the last time, at verse 169. So you can imagine how many visits the two elders made to the konsistorie altogether.

The last verse came, and the last line of the last verse. This time it had to be "Amen". Nothing could stop it. I would rather not describe the state that the congregation was in. And by then the three Native convicts, red stripes and all, were, in the Bakhatla tongue, threatening mutiny. "Aa-m-e-e-n" came from what sounded like less than a score of voices, hoarse with singing.

The organ music ceased.

Maybe it was the sudden silence that at last brought Dominee Welthagen out of his long trance. He raised his head and looked slowly about him. His gaze travelled over his congregation, and then, looking at the windows, he saw that it was night. We understood right away what was going on in Dominee Welthagen's mind. He thought he had just come into the pulpit, and that this was the beginning of the evening service. We realised that, during all the time we had been singing, the predikant had been in a state of unconsciousness.

Once again Dominee Welthagen took a firm grip on the pulpit rail. His head again started drooping forward on to his breast. But before he went into a trance for the second time, he gave the hymn for the evening service.

"We will," Dominee Welthagen announced, "sing Psalm 119."

NEWS STORY

"THE way the world is today," At Naudé said, shaking his head, "I don't know what is going to happen."

From that it was clear that At Naudé had been hearing news over the wireless again that made him fear for the future of the country. We did not exactly sit up, then. There was never any change, even in the kind of news he would bring us. Every time it was about stone-throwings in Johannesburg locations and about how many new kinds of bombs the Russians had got, and about how many people had gone to gaol for telling the Russians about still other kinds of bombs they could make. Although it did not look as though the Russians needed to be educated much in that line.

And we could never really understand why At Naudé listened at all. We hardly ever listened to him, for that matter. We would rather hear from Gysbert van Tonder if it was true that the ouderling at Pilansberg really forgot himself in the way that Jurie Steyn's wife had heard about from a kraal Mtosa at the kitchen door. The Mtosa had come to buy halfpenny stamps to stick on his forehead for the yearly Ndlolo dance. Now, there was news for you. About the ouderling, I mean. And even to hear that the Ndlolo dance was being held soon again was at least something. And if it should turn out that what was being said about the Pilansberg ouderling was not true, well, then, the same thing applied to a lot of what At Naudé heard over the wireless also.

"I don't know what is going to happen," At Naudé repeated, "the way the world is today. I just heard over the wireless . . .

"That's how the news we got in the old days was better," Oupa Bekker said. "I mean in the real old days, when there was no wireless, and there was not the telegraph, either. The news you got then you could do something with. And you didn't have to go

7

to the post office and get it from a newspaper. The post office is the curse of the Transvaal . . .

Jurie Steyn said that Oupa Bekker was quite right, there. He himself would never have taken on the job of postmaster at Drogevlei if he had as much as guessed that there were four separate forms that he would have to fill in, each of them different, just for a simple five-shilling money order. It would be so much brainier en neater, Jurie Steyn said, for people who wanted to send five shillings somewhere, if they would just wrap up a couple of half-crowns in a thick wad of brown paper and then post them in the ordinary way, like a letter. That was what the new red pillar-box in front of his door was for, Jurie Steyn explained. The authorities had gone to the expense of that new pillar-box in order to help the public. And yet you still found people coming in for postal orders and money orders. The other day a man even came in and asked could he telegraph some money, somewhere.

"I gave that man a piece of brown paper and showed him the pillar-box," Jurie Steyn said. "It seemed, until then, that he did not know what kind of progress we had been making here. I therefore asked him if I could show him some more ways in regard to how advanced the Groot Marico was getting. But he said, no, the indications I had already given him were plenty."

Jurie Steyn said that he thought it was handsome of the man to have spoken up for the Marico like that, seeing that he was quite a newcomer to these parts.

Because we never knew how long Jurie Steyn would be when once he got on the subject of his work, we were glad when Johnny Coen asked Oupa Bekker to explain some more to us about how they got news in the old days. We were all pleased, that is, except At Naudé, who had again tried to get in a remark but had got no further than to say that if we knew something we would all shiver in our veldskoens.

"How did we get news?" Oupa Bekker said, replying to another question of Johnny Coen's. "Well, you would be standing in the lands, say, and then one of the Bechuanas would point to a small cloud of dust in the poort, and you would walk across to the big tree by the dam, where the road bends, and the traveller would come past there, with two vos horses in front of his Cape-cart, and he would get off from the cart and shake hands and say he was Du Plessis. And you would say you were Bekker, and he would say, afterwards, that he couldn't stay the night on your farm, because he had to get to Tsalala's Kop. Well, there was news. You could talk about it for days. For weeks even. You have got no idea how often my wife and I discussed it. And we knew everything that there was to know about the man. We knew his name was Du Plessis."

At Naudé said, then, that he did not think much of that sort of news. People must have been a bit simpel in the head, in those old times that Oupa Bekker was talking about, if they thought anything of that sort of news. Why, if you compared it with what the radio announcer said, only yesterday . . .

Jurie Steyn's wife came in from the kitchen at that moment. There was a light of excitement in her eyes. And when she spoke it was to none of us in particular.

"It has just occurred to me," Jurie Steyn's wife said, "that is, if it's true what they are saying about the Pilansberg ouderling, of course. Well, it has just struck me that, when he forgot himself in the way they say — provided that he did forget himself like that, mind you — well, perhaps the ouderling didn't know that anybody was looking."

That was a possibility that had not so far occurred to us, and we discussed it at some length. In between our talk At Naudé was blurting out something about the rays from a still newer kind of bomb that would kill you right in the middle of the veld and through fifty feet of concrete. So, we said, of course, that the best thing to do would be to keep a pretty safe distance away from concrete, with those sort of rays about, if concrete was as dangerous as all that.

We were in no mood for foolishness. Oupa Bekker took this as an encouragement for him to go on.

"Or another day," Oupa Bekker continued, "you would again be standing in your lands, say, or sitting, even, if there was a long day of ploughing ahead, and you did not want to tire yourself out unnecessarily. You would be sitting on a stone in the shade of a tree, say, and you would think to yourself how lazy those Bechuanas look, going backwards and forwards, backwards and forwards, with the plough and the oxen, and you would get quite sleepy, say, thinking to yourself how lazy those Bechuanas are. If it wasn't for the oxen to keep them going, they wouldn't do any work at all, you might perhaps think.

"And then, without your in the least expecting it, you would again have news. And the news would find a stone for himself and come along and sit down right next to you. It would be the new veldkornet, say. And why nobody saw any dust in the poort, that time, was because the veldkornet didn't come along the road. And you would make a joke with him and say: 'I suppose that's why they call you a veldkornet, because you don't travel along the road, but you come by the veld-langers.' And the veldkornet would laugh and ask you a few questions, and he would tell you that they had had good rains at Derdepoort . . . Well, there was something that I could tell my wife over and over again, for weeks. It was news. For weeks I had that to think about. The visit of the veldkornet. In the old days it was real news."

We could see from the way At Naudé was fidgeting in his chair that he guessed we were just egging the old man on to talk, in order to scoff at all the important European news that he, At Naudé, regularly retailed to us, and that we were getting tired of.

After a while At Naudé could no longer contain himself.

"This second-childhood drivel that Oupa Bekker is talking," At Naudé announced, not looking at anybody in particular, but saying it to all of us, in the way Jurie Steyn's wife had spoken when she came out of the kitchen. "Well, I would actually sooner listen to scandal about the Pilansberg ouderling. There is at least some sort of meaning to it. I am not being unfriendly to Oupa Bekker, of course. I know it's just that he's old. But it's also quite clear to me that he doesn't know what news is, at all."

Jurie Steyn said that Oupa Bekker's news was at least more sensible than a man lying on the veld under fifty feet of concrete because of some rays. If a man were to lie under fifty feet of concrete, he wouldn't be able to breathe, leave alone anything else.

In the meantime, Johnny Coen had been asking Oupa Bekker to tell us some more.

"On another day, say," Oupa Bekker would go on, "you would not be in your lands at all, but you would be sitting on your front stoep, drinking coffee, say. And the Cape-cart with the two vos horses in front would be coming down the road again, but in the opposite direction, going towards the poort, this time. And you would not see much of Du Plessis's face, because his hat would be pulled over his eyes. And the veldkornet would be sitting on the Cape-cart next to him, say."

Oupa Bekker paused. He paused for quite a while, too, holding a lighted match cupped over his pipe as though he was out in the veld where there was wind, and puffing vigorously.

"And my wife and I would go on talking about it for years afterwards, say," Oupa Bekker went on. "For years after Du Plessis was hanged, I mean."

POTCHEFSTROOM WILLOW

"THE trouble," At Naudé said, "about getting the latest war news over the wireless, is that Klaas Smit and his Boeremusiek orchestra start up right away after it, playing 'Die Nooi van Potchefstroom'. Now, it isn't that I don't like that song—"

So we said that it wasn't as though we didn't like it, either. Gysbert van Tonder began to hum the tune. Johnny Coen joined in, singing the words softly — "Vertel my neef, vertel my oom, is dit die pad na Potchefstroom?" In a little while we were all singing. Not very loudly, of course. For Jurie Steyn was conscious of the fact that his post office was a public place, and he frowned on any sort of out-of- the-way behaviour in it. We still remembered the manner in which Jurie Steyn had spoken to Chris Welman the time Chris was mending a pair of his wife's veldskoens in the post office, using the corner of the counter as a last.

"I can't object to your sitting in my post office, waiting for the Government lorry," Jurie Steyn said, "as long as you're white. You're entitled to sit here. You're also entitled to drink the coffee that my wife is soft-hearted enough to bring round to you on a tray. I'm sure I don't know why she does it. I was in the post office in Johannesburg, once, and I didn't see anybody coming around there, with cups of coffee on a tray. If you wanted coffee in the Johannesburg post office you would have to go round to the kitchen door for it, I suppose. And I feel that's what my wife should do, also. But she doesn't. All right — she's soft hearted. But I won't let any man come and mend boots on my post office counter and right next to the official brass scales, too. I won't. If I allow that, the next thing a man will do is he'll come in here and sit down on my rusbank and read a book. We all know my voorkamer is a public place, but I will not let anybody take liberties in it."

For that reason, we did not raise our voices very much when

we sang "Die Nooi van Potchefstroom". But it was a catchy song, and Jurie Steyn joined in a little, too, afterwards.

Not that he let himself go in any way, of course. He sang in a reserved and dignified fashion, that made you feel he would yet go far. You felt that even the Postmaster General in Pretoria, on the occasion of a member of the public coming to him to complain about a registered letter that had got lost, say — well, even the Postmaster General would not have been able to sit back in his chair and sing "Die Nooi van Potchefstroom" in as elevated a manner as what Jurie Steyn was doing at that very moment.

Before the singing had quite died down, Oupa Bekker was saying that he knew Potchefstroom when he was still a child. It was in the very old days, Oupa Bekker said, and the far side foundations of the church on Kerkplein had not sunk nearly as deep as they had done today. He said he remembered the first time that there was a split in the Church. It was between the Doppers and the Hervormdes, he said. And it was quite a serious split. And because he was young, then, he thought it had to do with the way the brickwork on the wall nearest the street had to be constantly plastered up, from top to bottom, the more the foundations sank.

"I remember showing my father that piece of church wall," Oupa Bekker continued. "And I asked my father if the Doppers had done it. And my father said, well, he had never thought about it like that, until then. But all the same, he wouldn't be surprised if it was so. Not that anybody would ever see the Doppers kneeling down there on the sidewalk, loosening the bricks with a crowbar, my father added. The Doppers were too cunning for that. Whatever they did was under the cover of darkness."

At Naudé started talking again about the news of the war in Korea, that he had heard over the wireless. But because so much had been spoken in between, he had to explain right from the beginning again.

"It's the way the war news gets crowded by Klaas Smit and his orchestra," At Naudé said. "You're listening to what the announcer is making clear about what part of the country General

13

MacArthur is fighting in now — and it's had to follow all that, because it seems to me that sometimes General MacArthur himself is not too clear as to what part of the country he is in — and then, suddenly, while you're still listening, up strikes Klaas Smit's orchestra with 'Die Nooi van Potchefstroom'. It makes it all very difficult, you know. They don't give that General Mac- Arthur a chance at all. 'Die Nooi van Potchefstroom' seems to be crowding him even worse than the Communists are doing — and that seems to be bad enough, the Lord knows."

This time we did not start singing again. We had, after all, taken the song to the end, and even if it wasn't for Jurie Steyn's feelings, we ourselves knew enough about the right way of conducting ourselves in a post office. You can't go and sing the same song in a post office twice, just as though it's the quarterly meeting of the Mealie Control Board. We were glad, therefore, when Oupa Bekker started talking once more.

"This song, now," Oupa Bekker was saying. "Well, as you know, I remember the early days of Potchefstroom. The very early days, that is. But I would never have imagined that some day a poet would come along and make up a song about the place. Potchefstroom was the first capital of the Transvaal, of course. Long before Pretoria was thought of, even.

"And there's an old willow-tree in Potchefstroom that must have measured I don't know how many feet around the trunk where it goes into the ground. It measured that much only a little while ago, I mean. I am talking about the last time I was in Potchefstroom. But I never imagined anybody would ever write a poem about the town. It seemed such a hard name to make verses about. But I suppose it's a lot different today. People are so much more clever, I expect."

Johnny Coen, who had worked on the Railways in Ottoshoop and knew a good deal about culture, assured Oupa Bekker that that was indeed the case. For a poet that wanted to write poetry today, Johnny Coen said, there was no word that would put him off. In fact, the harder the word, the better the poet would like it.

Not that he knew anything about poetry himself, Johnny Coen acknowledged, but he had been round the world a bit, and he kept his eyes open, and he had seen a thing or two.

"If you saw the way they concreted up the buffers for the shunting engine on the goods line," Johnny Coen said, "then you would know what I was talking about. It was five-eighths steel reinforcements right through. After that, for a poet to make up a poem with the name of Potchefstroom in it, why, man, if you saw how they built up that extra platform all in box sections, you'll understand how it is that people have got the brains today to deal with problems that were a bit beyond them, no doubt, in Oupa Bekker's time."

Oupa Bekker nodded his head several times. He would have gone on nodding it a good deal longer, maybe, if it wasn't that Jurie Steyn's wife came in just about then with the coffee. Consequently, Oupa Bekker had to sit up properly and stir the sugar round in his cup.

"I heard that song you were singing, just now," Jurie Steyn's wife remarked to all of us. "I thought it was — well, I liked it. I didn't catch the words, quite."

Nobody answered. We knew that it was school holidays, of course. And we knew that young Vermaak, the schoolmaster, had gone to his parents in Potchefstroom for the holidays. Because we knew that Potchefstroom was young Vermaak's home town, we kept silent. There was no telling what Jurie Steyn's reactions would be.

Oupa Bekker went on talking, however.

"All the same, I would like to know how many feet around the trunk that willow-tree is today," Oupa Bekker said. "And they won't chop it down either. That willow tree is right on the edge of the graveyard. You can almost say it's inside the graveyard. And so they won't chop it down. But what beats me is to think that somebody could actually write a song about Potchefstroom. I would never have thought it possible."

Oupa Bekker's sigh seemed to come from very far away.

From somewhere a good deal further away than the rusbank he was sitting on. We understood then why that Potchefstroom willow-tree meant so much to him.

And the result was that when Gysbert van Tonder started up the chorus of that song again, we all found ourselves joining in — no matter what Jurie Steyn might say about it. "En in my droom," we sang, "Is die vaalhaarnooi by die wilgerboom."

BIRTH CERTIFICATE

IT was when At Naudé told us what he had read in the newspaper about a man who had thought all his life that he was White, and had then discovered that he was Coloured, that the story of Flippus Biljon was called to mind. I mean, we all knew the story of Flippus Biljon. But because it was still early afternoon we did not immediately make mention of Flippus. Instead, we discussed, at considerable length, other instances that were within our knowledge of people who had grown up as one sort of person and had discovered in later life that they were in actual fact quite a different sort of person.

Many of these stories that we recalled in Jurie Steyn's voorkamer as the shadows of the thorn-trees lengthened were based only on hearsay. It was the kind of story that you had heard, as a child, at your grandmother's knee. But your grandmother would never admit, of course, that she had heard that story at her grandmother's knee. Oh, no. She could remember very clearly how it all happened, just like it was yesterday. And she could tell you the name of the farm. And the name of the landdrost who was summoned to take note of the extraordinary occurrence, when it had to do with a more unusual sort of changeling, that is. And she would recall the solemn manner in which the landdrost took off his hat when he said that there were many things that were beyond human understanding.

Similarly now, in the voorkamer, when we recalled stories of white children that had been carried off by a Bushman or a baboon or a werewolf, even, and had been brought up in the wilds and without any proper religious instruction, then we also did not think it necessary to explain where we had first heard those stories. We spoke as though we had been actually present at some stage of the affair — more usually at the last scene, where the child, now grown to manhood and needing trousers and a pair of braces and a hat, gets restored to his parents, and the magistrate, after studying the birth certificate, says that there are things in this world that baffle the human mind.

And while the shadows under the thorn-trees grew longer, the stories we told in Jurie Steyn's voorkamer grew, if not longer, then, at least, taller.

"But this isn't the point of what I have been trying to explain," At Naudé interrupted a story of Gysbert van Tender's that was getting a bit confused in parts, through Gysbert van Tender not being quite clear as to what a werewolf was. "When I read that bit in the newspaper I started wondering how must a man feel, after he has grown up with adopted parents and he discovers, quite late in life, through seeing his birth certificate for the first time, that he isn't White, after all. That is what I am trying to get at. Supposing Gysbert were to find out suddenly—"

At Naudé pulled himself up short. Maybe there were one or two things about a werewolf that Gysbert van Tender wasn't too sure about, and he would allow himself to be corrected by Oupa Bekker on such points. But there were certain things he wouldn't stand for.

"All right," At Naudé said hastily, "I don't mean Gysbert van Tonder, specially. What I am trying to get at is, how would any one of us feel? How would any White man feel, if he has passed as White all his life, and he sees for the first time, from his birth certificate, that his grandfather was Coloured? I mean, how would he *feel*? Think of that awful moment when he looks in the palm of his hands and he sees . . ."

"He can have that awful moment," Gysbert van Tonder said. "I've looked at the palm of my hand. It's a White man's palm. And my finger-nails have also got proper half-moons."

At Naudé said he had never doubted that. No, there was no need for Gysbert van Tonder to come any closer and show him. He could see quite well enough just from where he was sitting. After Chris Welman had pulled Gysbert van Tonder back on to the rusbank by his jacket, counselling him not to do anything foolish, since At Naudé did not mean *him*, Oupa Bekker started talking about a White child in Schweizer-Reneke that had been stolen out of its cradle by a family of baboons.

"I haven't seen that cradle myself," Oupa Bekker acknowledged, modestly. "But I met many people who have. After the child had been stolen, neighbours from as far as the Orange River came to look at that cradle. And when they looked at it they admired the particular way that Heilart Nortjé — that was the child's father — had set about making his household furniture, with glued *klinkpenne* in the joints, and all. But the real interest about the cradle was that it was empty, proving that the child had been stolen by baboons. I remember how one neighbour, who was not on very good terms with Heilart Nortjé, went about the district saying that it could only have *been* baboons.

"But it was many years before Heilart Nortjé and his wife saw their child again. By saw, I mean getting near enough to be able to talk to him and ask him how he was getting on. For he was always too quick, from the way the baboons had brought him up. At intervals Heilart Nortjé and his wife would see the tribe of baboons sitting on a rant, and their son, young Heilart, would be in the company of the baboons. And once, through his field-glasses, Heilart had been able to observe his son for quite a few moments. His son was then engaged in picking up a stone and laying hold of a scorpion that was underneath it. The speed with which his son pulled off the scorpion's sting and proceeded to eat up the rest of the scorpion whole filled the father's heart of Heilart Nortjé with a deep sense of pride.

"I remember how Heilart talked about it. 'Real intelligence,' Heilart announced with his chest stuck out. 'A real baboon couldn't have done it quicker or better. I called my wife, but she was a bit too late. All she could see was him looking as pleased as anything and scratching himself. And my wife and I held hands and we smiled at each other and we asked each other, where does he get it all from?'

"But then there were times again when that tribe of baboons would leave the Schweizer-Reneke area and go deep into the Kalahari, and Heilart Nortjé and his wife would know nothing about what was happening to their son, except through reports from farmers near whose homesteads the baboons had passed. Those farmers had a lot to say about what happened to some of their sheep, not to talk of their mealies and watermelons. And Heilart would be very bitter about those farmers. Begrudging his son a few prickly pears, he said.

"And it wasn't as though he hadn't made every effort to get his son back, Heilart said, so that he could go to catechism classes, since he was almost of age to be confirmed. He had set all sorts of traps for his son, Heilart said, and he had also thought of shooting the baboons, so that it would be easier, after that, to get his son back. But there was always the danger, firing into a pack like that, of his shooting his own son.

"The neighbour that I have spoken of before," Oupa Bekker continued, "who was not very well disposed towards Heilart Nortjé, said that the real reason Heilart didn't shoot was because he didn't always know — actually know — which was his son and which was one of the more flat-headed *kees*-baboons."

It seemed that this was going to be a very long story. Several of us started getting restive . . . So Johnny Coen asked Oupa Bekker, in a polite sort of a way, to tell us how it all ended.

"Well, Heilart Nortjé caught his son, afterwards," Oupa Bekker said. "But I am not sure if Heilart was altogether pleased about it. His son was so hard to tame. And then the way he caught him. It was with the simplest sort of baboon trap of all . . . Yes, that one. A calabash with a hole in it just big enough for you to put your hand in, empty, but that you can't get your hand out of again when you're clutching a fistful of mealies that was put at the bottom of the calabash. Heilart Nortjé never got over that, really. He felt it was a very shameful thing that had happened to him. The thought that his son, in whom he had taken so much pride, should have allowed himself to be caught in the simplest form of monkey-trap."

When Oupa Bekker paused, Jurie Steyn said that it was indeed a sad story, and it was no doubt perfectly true. There was just a certain tone in Jurie Steyn's voice that made Oupa Bekker continue.

"True in every particular," Oupa Bekker declared, nodding his head a good number of times. "The landdrost came over to see about it, too. They sent for the landdrost so that he could make a report about it. I was there, that afternoon, in Heilart Nortjé's voorkamer, when the landdrost came. And there were a good number of other people, also. And Heilart Nortjé's, son, half-tamed in some ways but still baboon-wild in others, was there also. The landdrost studied the birth certificate very carefully. Then the landdrost said that what he had just been present at surpassed ordinary human understanding. And the landdrost took off his hat in a very solemn fashion.

"We all felt very embarrassed when Heilart Nortjé's son grabbed the hat out of the landdrost's hand and started biting pieces out of the crown."

When Oupa Bekker said those words it seemed to us like the end of a story. Consequently, we were disappointed when At Naudé started making further mention of that piece of news he had read in the daily paper. So there was nothing else for it but that we had to talk about Flippus Biljon. For Flippus Biljon's case was just the opposite of the case of the man that At Naudé's newspaper wrote about.

Because he had been adopted by a Coloured family, Flippus Biljon had always regarded himself as a Coloured man. And then one day, quite by accident, Flippus Biljon saw his birth certificate. And from that birth certificate it was clear that Flippus Biljon was as White as you or I. You can imagine how Flippus Biljon must have felt about it. Especially after he had gone to see the magistrate at Bekkersdal, and the magistrate, after studying the birth certificate, confirmed the fact that Flippus Biljon was a White man.

"Thank you, *baas*," Flippus Biljon said. "Thank you very much, my *basie*."

PLAY WITHIN A PLAY

"BUT what did Jacques le Français want to put a thing like that on for?" Gysbert van Tonder asked.

In those words, he conveyed something of what we all felt about the latest play with which the famous Afrikaans actor, Jacques le Français, was touring the platteland. A good number of us had gone over to Bekkersdal to attend the play. But — as always happens in such cases — those who hadn't actually seen the play knew just as much about it as those who had. More, even, sometimes.

"What I can't understand is how the kerkraad allowed Jacques le Français to hire the church hall for a show like that," Chris Welman said. "Especially when you think that the church hall is little more than a stone's throw from the church itself."

Naturally, Jurie Steyn could not let that statement pass. Criticism of the church council implied also a certain measure of fault-finding with Deacon Kirstein, who was a first cousin of Jurie's wife.

"You can hardly call it a stone's throw," Jurie Steyn declared. "After all, the plein is on two morgen of ground and the church hall is at the furthest end from the church itself. And there is also a row of blue-gums in between. Tall, well-grown blue-gums. No, you can hardly call all that a stone's throw, Chris."

So At Naudé said that what had no doubt happened was that Jacques le Français with his insinuating play-actor ways had got round the members of the kerkraad, somehow. With lies, as likely as not. Maybe he had told the deacons and elders that he was going to put on that play "Ander Man se Kind" again, which everybody approved of, seeing it was so instructive, the relentless way in which it showed up the sinful life led in the great city of Johannesburg, and in which the girl in the play, Baba Haasbroek, got ensnared, because she was young and from the backveld, and didn't know any better.

"Although I don't know if that play did any good, really," At Naudé added, thoughtfully. "I mean, it was shortly after that that Drieka Basson of Enzelsberg left for Johannesburg, wasn't it? Perhaps the play 'Ander Man se Kind' was a bit too — well — relentless."

Thereupon Johnny Coen took a hand in the conversation. It seemed very long ago, the time Johnny Coen had gone to Johannesburg because of a girl that was alone there in that great city. And on his return to the Marico, he had not spoken much of his visit, beyond mentioning that there were two men carved in stone holding up the doorway of a building near the station and that the pavements were so crowded that you could hardly walk on them. But for a good while after that he had looked more lonely in Jurie Steyn's voorkamer than any stranger could look in a great city.

"I don't know if you can say that that play of Jacques le Français's about the girl that went to Johannesburg really is so very instructive," Johnny Coen said. "There are certain things in it that are very true, of course. But there are also true things that could never go into one of Jacques le Français's plays — or into any play, I think."

Gysbert van Tonder started to laugh, then. It was a short sort of a laugh.

"I remember what you said when you came back from Johannesburg, that time," Gysbert van Tonder said to Johnny Coen. "You said the pavements were so crowded that there was hardly room to walk. Well, in the play 'Ander Man se Kind' it wasn't like that. The girl in the play, Baba Haasbroek, didn't seem to have trouble to walk about on the pavement. I mean, half the time, in the play, she was walking on the pavement. Or if she wasn't walking, she was standing under a street lamp."

It was then that At Naudé mentioned the girl in the new play that Jacques le Français had put on at Bekkersdal. Her name was

23

Truida Ziemers. It was a made-up name, of course, At Naudé said. Just like Jacques le Français was a made-up name. His real name was Poggenpoel, or something. But how any Afrikaans writer could write a thing like that . . .

"It wasn't written by an Afrikaans dramatist," young Vermaak, the school-teacher, explained. "It is a translation from . . ."

"To think that any Afrikaner should fall so low as to translate a thing like that, then," Gysbert van Tonder interrupted him. "And what's more, Jacques le Français or Jacobus Poggenpoel, or whatever his name is, is Coloured. I could see he was Coloured. No matter how he tried to make himself up, and all, to look White, it was a Coloured man walking about there on the stage. How I didn't notice it in the play 'Ander Man se Kind' I don't know. Maybe I sat too near the back, that time."

Young Vermaak did not know, of course, to what extent we were pulling his leg. He shook his head sadly. Then he started to explain, in a patient sort of a way, that Jacques le Français was actually playing the role of a Coloured man. He wasn't supposed to be White. It was an important part in the unfolding of the drama that Jacques le Français wasn't a White man. It told you all that in the title of the play, the schoolmaster said.

"What's he then, a Frenchman?" Jurie Steyn asked. "Why didn't they say so, straight out?"

Several of us said after that, each in turn, that there was something you couldn't understand, now. That a pretty girl like Truida Ziemers, with a blue flower in her hat, should fall in love with a Coloured man, and even marry him. Because that was what happened in the play.

"And it wasn't as though she didn't know," Chris Welman remarked. "Meneer Vermaak has just told us that it says it in the title of the play, and all. Of course, I didn't see the play myself. I meant to go, but at the last moment one of my mules took sick. But I saw Truida Ziemers on the stage, once. And even now, as I am talking about her again, I can remember how pretty she was. And to think that she went and married a Coloured man when all the time she knew. And it wasn't as though he could tell her that it was just sunburn, seeing that she could read it for herself on the posters. If the schoolmaster could read it, so could Truida."

Anyway, that was only to be expected, Gysbert van Tonder said. That Jacques le Français would murder Truida Ziemers in the end, he meant. After all, what else could you expect from a marriage like that? Maybe from that point of view the play could be taken as a warning to every respectable White girl in the country.

"But that isn't the point of the play," young Vermaak insisted, once more. "Actually, it is a good play. And it is a play with real educational value. But not that kind of educational value. If I tell you that this play is a translation (and a pretty poor translation, too: I wouldn't be surprised if Jacques le Français translated it himself) of the work of the great . . ."

This time the interruption came from Johnny Coen.

"It's all very well talking like they have been doing about a girl going wrong," Johnny Coen said. "But a great deal depends on circumstances. That is something I have learnt, now. Take the case now of a girl that . . ."

We all sat up to listen, then. And Gysbert van Tonder nudged Chris Welman in the ribs for coughing. We did not wish to miss a word.

"A girl that . . .?" At Naudé repeated in a tone of deep understanding, to encourage Johnny Coen to continue.

"Well, take a girl like that girl Baba Haasbroek in the play 'Ander Man se Kind'," Johnny Coen said. Jurie Steyn groaned. We didn't want to hear all that, over again.

"Well, anyway, if that girl did go wrong," Johnny Coen proceeded — pretty diffidently, now, as though he could sense our feelings of being balked — "then there might be reasons for it. Reasons that didn't come out in the play, maybe. And reasons that we sitting here in Jurie Steyn's voorkamer would perhaps not have the right to judge about, either."

Gysbert van Tonder started clearing his throat as though for another short laugh. But he seemed to change his mind half-way through.

"And in this last play, now," Johnny Coen added, "if Jacques le Français had really loved the girl, he wouldn't have been so jealous."

"Yes, it's a pity that Truida Ziemers got murdered in the end, like that," At Naudé remarked. "Her friends in the play should have seen what Jacques le Français was up to, and have put the police on to him, in time."

He said that with a wink, to draw young Vermaak, of course.

Thereupon the schoolmaster explained with much serious-ness that such an ending would defeat the whole purpose of the drama. But by that time, we had lost all interest in the subject. And when the Government lorry came soon afterwards and blew a lot of dust in at the door, we made haste to collect our letters and milk-cans.

Consequently, nobody took much notice of what young Ver-maak went on to tell us about the man who wrote the play. Not the man who translated it into Afrikaans, but the man who wrote it in the first place. He was a writer who used to hold horses' heads in front of a theatre, the schoolmaster said, and when he died, he left his second-best bed to his wife, or something.

STARS IN THEIR COURSES

"IT said over the wireless," At Naudé announced, "that the American astronomers are moving out of Johannesburg. I hey are taking the telescopes and things they have been studying the stars with, to Australia. There is too much smoke in Johannesburg for them to be able to see the stars properly."

He paused, as though inviting comment. But none of us had anything to say. We weren't interested in the Americans and their stars. Or in Australia, either, much.

"The American astronomers have been in Johannesburg for many years," At Naudé went on, wistfully, as though the impending removal of the astronomical research station was a matter of personal regret to him. "They have been here for years and now they are going, because of the smoke. It gets into their eyes just when they have nearly seen a new star in their telescopes, I suppose. Well, smoke is like that, of course. It gets into your eyes just at the wrong time."

What At Naudé had said now was something that we could all understand. It was something of which we had all had experience. It was different from what he had been saying before about eyepieces and refracting telescopes, that he had heard of over the wireless, and that he had got all wrong, no doubt. Whereas getting smoke in your eyes at an inconvenient moment was something everybody in the Marico understood.

Immediately, Chris Welman started telling us about the time he was asked by Koos Nienaber, as a favour, to stand on a rant of the Dwarsberge from where he was able to see the Derdepoort police post very clearly. Koos Nienaber, it would seem, had private business with a chief near Ramoutsa, which had to do with bringing a somewhat large herd of cattle with long horns across the border.

"I could see the police post very well from there," Chris Welman said. "I was standing near a Mtosa hut. When the Mtosa woman lifted a petrol tin on to her head and went down in the direction of the spruit, for water, I moved over to an iron pot that a fire had been burning underneath all afternoon. All afternoon it had smelt to me like sheep's inside and kaboe mealies. And when Koos Nienaber had asked me to do that small favour for him, of standing on the rant and watching if the two policemen just went on dealing out cards to each other and taking turns to drink out of a black bottle, Koos Nienaber had forgotten to give me something to take along that I could eat."

He could still see those two policemen quite distinctly, Chris Welman said, when he lifted the lid off the iron pot. He wasn't in the least worried about those two policemen, then. Actually, he admitted that he was, if anything, more concerned lest that Mtosa woman should suddenly come back to the hut, with the petrol tin on her head, having forgotten something. And it had to be at that moment, just when he was lifting the lid, that smoke from the fire crackling underneath the pot got into his eyes. It was the most awful kind of stabbing smoke that you could ever imagine, Chris Welman said. What the Mtosa woman had made that fire with, he just had no idea. Cow-dung and bitter-bessie he knew. That was a kind of fuel that received some countenance, still, in the less frequented areas along the Malopo. And it made a kind of smoke which, if it got into your eyes, could blind you temporarily for up to at least quarter of an hour.

Chris Welman went on to say that he was also not unfamiliar with the effects of the smoke from the arnosterbos, in view of the fact that he retained many childhood memories of a farm in the Eastern Province, where it was still quite usual to find a house with an old-fashioned *abba-* kitchen.

It was obvious that Chris Welman was beginning to yield to a gentle mood of reminiscence. The next thing, he would be telling us some of the clever things that he was able to say at the age of four. Several of us pulled him up short, then.

"All right," Chris Welman proceeded, "I think I know how you feel. Well, to get back to that rant where I was standing on — well, I don't know what kind of fuel it was under that iron pot. What I will never forget is the moment when that smoke got into my eyes. It was a kind of smart that you couldn't rub out with the back of your sleeve or with the tail of your shirt pulled up, even. I don't think that even one of those white handkerchiefs that you see in the shop windows in Zeerust would have helped much. All I know is that when some of the pain started going, and I was able to see a little bit, again, I was lying under a 'mdubu-tree half-way down that rant. I had been running around in circles for I don't know how long. And it might give you some sort of an idea of the state I was in, if I tell you that I discovered, then, that I had been carrying that pot lid around with me all the time. I have often wondered if the Mtosa woman ever found that lid, lying there under the 'mdubu. And if she did, what she thought."

Chris Welman sighed deeply. Partly, we felt, that sigh had its roots in a nostalgia for the past. His next words showed, however, that it was linked with a grimmer sort of reality.

"When I got back to the top of that rant," Chris Welman declared simply, "the two policemen weren't there at the post any more. And Koos Nienaber had been fined so often before that this time the magistrate would not let him off with a fine. Koos Nienaber took it like a man, though, when the magistrate gave him six months."

More than one of us, sitting in Jurie Steyn's voorkamer, sighed, too, then. We also knew what it was to get smoke in your eyes, at the wrong moment. We also knew what it was to hold sudden and unexpected converse with a policeman on border patrol, the while you were nervously shifting a pair of wire-cutters from one hand to the other.

Gysbert van Tender brought the discussion back to the subject of the stars.

"If the American astronomers are leaving South Africa because they can't stand our sort of smoke," Gysbert van Tonder declared, "well, I suppose there's nothing we can do about it. Maybe they haven't got smoke in America. I don't know, of course. But I didn't think that an astronomer, watching the stars at night through a telescope, would worry very much about smoke — or about cinders from looking out of a train window, either — getting into his eyes. I imagined that an astronomer would be above that sort of thing."

Young Vermaak, the school-teacher, was able to put Gysbert van Tender right then. In general, of course, we never had much respect for the school-teacher, seeing that all he had was book-learning and didn't know, for instance, a simple thing like that an ystervark won't roll himself up when he's tame.

"It isn't the smoke that gets into their eyes," the schoolteacher explained. "It's the smoke in the atmosphere that interferes with the observations and mathematical calculations that the astronomers have to make to get a knowledge of the movements of the heavenly bodies. There's Tycho Brahe and Galileo, for one thing, and there's Newton and the mass of the sun in tons. And there's Betelgeuse in the constellation of Orion and the circumference of the moon's orbit. The weight of a terrestrial pound on the moon is two-and-a-half ounces and the speed of Uranus round the sun is I forget how many hundred thousand miles a day — hundred thousand miles, mind you."

We looked at each other, then; with feelings of awe. We were not so much impressed with the actual figures, of course, that the schoolmaster quoted. We could listen to all that and not as much as turn a hair. Like when the schoolmaster spoke about the density of the sun, reckoning the earth as 1.25, we were not at all overwhelmed. We were only surprised that it was not more. Or when the schoolmaster said that the period of the sun's rotation on its axis was 25 days and something — that didn't flatten us out in the least. It could be millions of years, for all we cared; millions and millions of years — that couldn't shake us. But what did give us pause for reflection was the thought that just in his brain — just inside his head, that didn't seem very much different from any one of our heads — the young schoolmaster should have so much knowledge.

When the schoolmaster had gone on to speak about curved shapes and about the amount of heat and light received by the other planets being as follows, we were rendered pretty well speechless. Only Jurie Steyn was not taken out of his depth.

"It's like that book my wife used to study a great deal before we got married," Jurie Steyn said. "I have told you about it before. It's called Napoleon's dream book. Well, that's a lot like what young Vermaak has been talking about now. At the back of the Napoleon dream book it's got 'What the Stars Foretell' for every day of the year. It says that on Wednesday you must wear green, and on some other day you must write a letter to a relative that you haven't seen since I don't know when. Anyway, I suppose that's why those American star-gazers are leaving Johannesburg. It's something they saw in the stars, I expect."

Chris Welman said he wondered if what the American astronomers saw through their telescope said that the star of the American nation was going up, or if it was going down.

"Perhaps Jurie Steyn's wife can work it out from the dream book," Gysbert van Tender said.

LOST CITY

"IT used to be different, in the Kalahari," Chris Welman said, commenting on At Naudé's announcement of what he had heard over the wireless. "You could go for miles and miles, and it would be just desert. All you'd come across, perhaps, would be a couple of families of Bushmen, and they'd be disappearing over the horizon. Then, days later, you'd again come across a couple of families of Bushmen. And they'd be disappearing over the horizon.

"And you wouldn't know if it was the same couple of families of Bushmen. Or the same horizon. And you wouldn't care either. I mean, in the Kalahari desert you wouldn't care. Maybe in other deserts it is different. I'm only talking about the Kalahari."

Yes, all you would be concerned about, in the Kalahari, Jurie Steyn said, was what the couple of families of Bushmen would be disappearing over the horizon with. For you might not always be able to check up quickly to find out what was missing out of your camp.

"But from what At Naudé has been telling us," Chris Welman went on, "it looks like you'd have no quiet in the Kalahari today. Or room to move. From Molepolole onwards it seems that there's just one expedition on top of another, each one searching for a lost city. And you can't slip out for a glass of pontac, even, in case when you come back somebody else has taken your place in the line."

It was apparent that Chris Welman was drawing on his memory of some past unhappy trip to Johannesburg.

It was not hard to think of how a city got lost in the first place, Jurie Steyn observed. "It must have been that the people that built the city didn't know what a couple of families of Bushmen were like. Still, I can't believe it, somehow, quite. Not a whole city, that is. I can't somehow imagine Bushmen disappearing over the horizon with all that. For one thing, it wouldn't be any use to them. Now if it wasn't so much a question of a whole lost city, but of some of the things that got lost out of the city — well, I could tell those expeditions just where to go and look."

But At Naudé said that we had perhaps misunderstood one or two of the less important details of the news he had communicated to us. There weren't quite as many expeditions as what Chris Welman seemed to think, out in the Kalahari looking for a lost city. Moreover, it wasn't a city that had got lost in the way that Jurie Steyn meant by lost. The city had just been built so many years ago that people had afterwards forgotten about it. Don't ask him how a thing like that could happen, now, At Naudé said. He admitted that he couldn't imagine it, himself.

"I mean, let's not take even a city—" At Naudé started to explain.

"No, let a few Bushman families take it," Jurie Steyn said, promptly, "with the washing hanging on the clotheslines and all."

"Not a city, even," At Naudé continued, pointedly ignoring Jurie Steyn's second attempt that afternoon at being what he thought funny, "but if we think of quite a small town, like Bekkersdal, say... Not that I won't agree that we've got a wider water-furrow in the main street of Bekkersdal than they've got in Zeerust, of course, but it's only that there are less people in the main street of Bekkersdal than they've got in Zeerust, if you understand what I mean . . . Well, can you imagine anybody in Bekkersdal forgetting where they built the place? After all, anybody can see for himself how silly that sounds. It's like Dominee Welthagen, just before the Nagmaal, suddenly forgetting where the church is. Or David Policansky not remembering where his shop is, just after he's done it all up for the New Year."

We acknowledged that At Naudé was right there, of course. With Dominee Welthagen we might not perhaps be too sure. For it was known that in some respects the dominee could at times be pretty absent-minded. But with David Policansky, At Naudé was on safe enough ground. Especially after that big new plate-glass window that David Policansky had put in. It was not reasonable to think that he would be able to forget it. Not with what he was still likely to be owing on it, we said. You just weren't allowed to forget anything you were owing on.

"So you see how much more silly it is with a city, then," At Naudé concluded. "Thinking that people would go and build a city, and then just lose it."

Thereupon young Vermaak, the schoolmaster, said that he had learnt in history of how for many centuries people believed that there was a foreign city called Monomotapa in these parts, and that numbers of expeditions had been sent out in the past to look for it. It was even marked on maps, long ago, the schoolmaster said. But if you saw that name on a map of Africa today, he said, well, then you would know that it wasn't a very up-to-date map of Africa.

As likely as not, there would not be the town of Vanderbijl Park marked on that map, young Vermaak said, laughing. Or the town of Odendaalsrus, even. There was supposed to be a lot of gold and diamonds in that city with the foreign name, the schoolmaster added.

Well, with those remarks young Vermaak broached a subject with which we were not altogether unfamiliar. More than one of us had, before today, held in his hand a map showing as clearly as anything with a cross the exact spot where the hidden treasure would be found buried. And all we'd be likely to dig up there would be an old jam-tin. The apocryphal element in African cartography was something we had had experience of.

"All I can say," Gysbert van Tonder observed at this stage, "is that I don't know so much about a lost city. But it seems to me there's going to be more than one lost expedition. Depending on how far the expeditions are going into the desert beyond Kang-Kang."

Several of us looked surprised when Gysbert van Tonder said that. Surprised and also impressed. We knew that in his time Gysbert van Tonder had penetrated pretty deeply into the Kalahari, bartering beads and brass wire for cattle. That was, of course, before the Natives in those parts found that they didn't need those things, any more, since they could buy their clothes ready-made at the Indian store at Ramoutsa. Nevertheless, we had not imagined that he had gone as far into the desert as all that.

"But is there—" Jurie Steyn enquired after a pause, "is there really a place by that name, though?"

Gysbert van Tonder smiled.

"On the map, yes," he said, "it is. On the map in my youngest son's school atlas you can read that name for yourself there, big as anything. And in the middle of the Kalahari. Well, there's something one of those expeditions can go and look for. And maybe that is their lost city. At least, it's lost enough. Because you certainly won't be able to tell it from any other spot in the Kalahari that you're standing in the middle of, watching a couple of families of Bushmen disappearing over the horizon from."

So Jurie Steyn said, yes, he reckoned that if it was a lost city that an expedition was after, why, then he reckoned that just about any part of the Kalahari would do for that. Because when the expedition came back from the Kalahari without having found anything, it would prove to the whole world just how lost that city actually was, Jurie Steyn reckoned. If that was what an expedition into the Kalahari was for, then that expedition just couldn't go wrong. In fact, the less that an expedition like that found, then, the better. Because it would show that the city had been lost without as much as a trace, even, Jurie Steyn added.

"It's a queer thing, though," the schoolmaster said, "when you come to think of it, that for so many hundreds of years, when the interior of South Africa was still unexplored, there should have been a legend of a Golden City. And people were so convinced of the existence of this city that they went searching for it. They were so sure that there was that city of gold that they even marked it on their maps. And what seems so extraordinary to me is that one day the Golden City actually would arise, and not too far away, either, from where the old geographers had centuries before indicated on their maps. It was as though they were all prophesying the rise of Johannesburg. And at most they were only a few hundred miles out."

That men should have been able to mark on a map, centuries beforehand, a city that was not there yet. That to him was one of the mysteries of Africa, the schoolmaster declared.

Thereupon Oupa Bekker said that if it was a thing like that that the schoolmaster thought wonderful, then the schoolmaster had a lot to learn, still.

"After all, with South Africa so big," Oupa Bekker said, "they were bound to go and build cities in it, somewhere. That stands to reason. And so, for a person to go and put a mark on a map and to say that some day there is going to be a city there, or thereabouts — well, what would have been wonderful was if it didn't work out, some time. And to say that it's surprising how that man made that mark on the map centuries ago, even. Well, I think that only shows how bad he was at it. If Johannesburg got started soon after he had prophesied it, then there might have been something in it, then. But it seems to me that the man who made that map wasn't only a few hundred miles out, as Meneer Vermaak says, but that he was also a few hundred years out. What's more, he also got the name wrong. Unless you also think that that name — what's it, again—"

"Monomotapa," young Vermaak announced.

"— isn't far out from sounding like Johannesburg," Oupa Bekker said.

It made him think of his grand-uncle Toons, all this, Oupa Bekker said. Now, there was something that really did come as a surprise to us. The general feeling we had about Oupa Bekker was a feeling of immense antiquity, of green and immemorial age. In the lost olden-time cities that our talk was about we could, without thinking twice, accord to Oupa Bekker the rights of a venerable citizenship. And in that crumbled town we could conceive of Oupa Bekker as walking about in the evening, among cobwebbed monuments. He seemed to belong with the battered though timeless antique.

It was foolish, of course, to have ideas like that. But that was the impression, in point of appearance and personality, that Oupa Bekker did make on us.

And so when Oupa Bekker spoke of himself as having had a grand-uncle, it just about took our breath away.

"You were saying about your grand-uncle?" Jurie Steyn, who was the first to recover, remarked. From the tone in his voice, you could see that Jurie Steyn pictured Oupa Bekker's grand-uncle as a lost city in himself, with weeds clambering over his ruined walls.

"My grand-uncle Toons," Oupa Bekker continued, unaware of the stir he had caused, "also had the habit, when he first trekked into the Transvaal, that was all just open veld, then, of stopping every so often and looking around him and saying that one day a great city would arise right there where he was standing, where it was now just empty veld. On his way up, when he trekked into the Northern Transvaal, he stopped to say it at where there is today Potchefstroom, and also at where there is today Johannesburg and Pretoria. In that way you could say that he was just as good as the man that did that map. And I suppose he was, too. That is, if you don't count all those hundreds of other places where my grand-uncle Toons also stopped to say the same thing, and where there is today still just open veld."

It was Jurie Steyn who brought the conversation back to where we had started from.

"Those expeditions going to search for the lost city," he asked of At Naudé, "have they set out yet? And do you know if they are likely to pass this way, at all? Because, if it's last letters they want to send home, and so on, then my post office is as good as any. I mean, their last letters have got a good chance of getting to where they are addressed to. I don't say the expeditions have got the same chance of getting to the lost city. But instead of taking all that trouble, why don't they just drop a letter in the post to the lost city — writing to the mayor, say? Then they'll at least know if the lost city is there or not."

But At Naudé said that from what he had heard over the wireless the expeditions were on the point of leaving, or had already left, Johannesburg. And as for what Jurie Steyn had said about writing letters — well, he had the feeling that more than one letter that he had himself posted had ended up there, in that lost city.

"Johannesburg?" Oupa Bekker queried, talking as though he was emerging from a dream. "Well, I've been in Johannesburg only a few times. Like with the Show, say. And I've passed through there on the way to Cape Town. And I've always tried to pull down the curtains of the compartment I was in when we went through Johannesburg. And I have thought of the Good Book, then.

"And I have thought that if ever there was a lost city, it was Johannesburg, I have thought. And *how lost*, I have thought... The expedition doesn't need to leave Johannesburg, if it's a lost city it wants."

FIVE-POUND NOTES

"IT explains in the newspaper how you can tell," At Naudé said, "the difference between a good five-pound note and these forged ones. There are a lot of forged notes in circulation, the paper says, and the police are on the point of making an arrest."

"Bad as all that, is it?" Gysbert van Tender asked. "Because I've noticed that when the papers say that about the police, it means that unless somebody walks into the charge office to confess that he did it, the police are writing that case off as an unsolved African mystery. There's only one thing worse, and that is when it says in the papers about a dragnet, and that the police are poised ready to swoop. That means that the guilty person left the country a good while before with a lot of luggage that he didn't have when he came into the country, and with his passport in order."

Gysbert van Tender's lip curled as he spoke. It was sad to think that an occasional misunderstanding with a mounted man on border patrol should have led to his acquiring so jaundiced a view of the activities of the forces charged with the state's internal government.

"Yes, I know," Chris Welman interjected. "It's because the forged note is twice the size of the genuine bank-note. And it's not properly printed, but is drawn just on a rough piece of brown paper with school crayons. And the lion on the back of it has got a pipe in his mouth.

"Oh, yes, and another thing — the portrait of Jan van Riebeeck is all wrong. Because Jan van Riebeeck is wearing a cap pulled down over one eye and a striped jersey with numbers on it. From that you can tell that the forger is in goal, and he's forging five-pound notes just from memory, and he's forgotten that striped jerseys with numbers on isn't the way everybody dresses. If somebody hands you a five-pound note like that, you must just say you're sorry you haven't got change.

"Because it's quite possible that the person is entirely innocent and is giving you the note in good faith. He might have got it from somebody else, and hadn't noticed that there was anything wrong with it."

Chris Welman's broad wink passed undetected by Jurie Steyn. Chris Welman was busy pulling At Naudé's leg, and Jurie Steyn didn't know it.

"In good faith" Jurie Steyn repeated. "Why, if a man came and palmed a piece of nonsense like that off on to me, just drawn with crayons on a piece of brown paper, I'd know straight away he was a crook. Never mind the lion with the pipe or the striped jersey, even. Just because it wasn't printed, I'd know it was a forgery. I'd be very suspicious of a man who came to me to change a five-pound note for him that was drawn by hand, however neatly. And I wouldn't care who that man was, either.

"Even if it was Dominee Welthagen himself that came along to me with that class of bank-note, I'd start getting funny ideas about what Dominee Welthagen was doing in his spare time. No matter how reverently Dominee Welthagen might speak about accepting the lion with the pipe in his mouth in good faith, either."

Young Vermaak, the schoolmaster, said that this was giving him something to think about. It would be a new subject for a composition for the children in the higher classes. The adventures of a shilling, passing from hand to hand, was a subject he had already set several times, and the children enjoyed writing it. But one got bored with having the same thing too often.

"The adventures of a spurious bank-note" would introduce a desirable element of novelty into school essays, he thought. Young Vermaak went on to say another thing that nobody in Jurie Steyn's voorkamer seemed to get the hang of, quite. He said that if the poet's purse was filled with the kind of brown-paper, crayon-executed bank-notes that Chris Welman had been talking about, then he could understand what the poet meant when he said that who stole his purse stole trash.

"How you can tell," At Naudé continued patiently, "that it is a counterfeit five-pound note is not, either, because on the picture of the ship the sailors are all standing round watching the captain doing card tricks. I mean, if Chris Welman wants to say ridiculous things, well, so can I. But the point is that it is actually a very good imitation note. The only way you can tell it's a forgery is that it is better printed than the genuine note and that it's got the word 'geoutoriseerde' spelt right."

The schoolmaster looked interested.

"Well, they keep on changing Afrikaans spelling so much," he said, "that I don't know where I am, half the time, teaching it. Anyway, I'd be glad to know what is the right way to spell that word. But, unfortunately, I haven't got a five-pound note on me at the moment — and I don't suppose there's anybody here who would care to lend me one."

His tone was pensive, wistful. But he was quite right. Nobody took the hint.

"Just until the end of the month," young Vermaak said again, but not very hopefully.

After an interval of silence, At Naudé said that even if somebody were to lend the schoolmaster a fiver — which, in his own opinion, did not seem very likely — it would still not help him with the spelling of that word. Because it was the genuine banknote that had the spelling wrong — spelling it the old way. Only the counterfeit note had the correct new spelling.

"I mean, if somebody here were to lend you a fiver," At Naudé said, trying to be funny again, since Chris Welman had started it, "I suppose it would be an honest fiver. I mean, I know that there are a lot of things that a Groot Marico cattle farmer will get up to — especially in a time of drought — but I don't think that printing counterfeit banknotes at the back of a haystack is one of them."

But Jurie Steyn said there was something that got him beat, now. Calling it a counterfeit note, Jurie Steyn said, just because it had better printing and spelling than a genuine note. It was one of those things that just made his head reel, Jurie Steyn added. No wonder a person sometimes felt in the world that he didn't know where he was. That was one of those things that made him feel, sometimes, that the Government was going too far. It was setting a pace that the ordinary citizen couldn't catch up with, quite.

"Saying that just because it's better than a real note," Jurie Steyn continued, "then for that reason, it's no good. That's got me floored, all right.

"By and by it will mean that if a respectably dressed stranger comes here to my post office, driving an expensive motor-car," Jurie Steyn said, "and he hands me a banknote that I can see nothing wrong with, except that it looks properly printed, then it means I'll have to notify the police at Nietverdiend. But if a Mshangaan in a blanket comes round here and he doesn't buy stamps, even, but he just wants change for a five-pound note, then I'll know it's all right, because the bank-note has got bad spelling and the lion on the back is rubbed out in places, through the pipe in his mouth having been drawn wrong the first time."

Oupa Bekker nodded his head up and down, thoughtfully, a few times. Yes, there were certain matters relative to currency as passed from person to person that did not always admit of facile comprehension, he said.

"Take the time the Stellaland Republic issued its own bank-notes, now," Oupa Bekker said. "Well, of course, the Stellaland Republic didn't last very long. And it might have been different if it had gone on a while. But I am just talking about how it was when we first got our own Stellaland Republic bank-notes, and of about how pleased we all were about it.

"For the trouble in that part of the country was that there were never enough gold coins to go round, properly. Even before the Stellaland Republic was set up, there was that trouble. You could notice it easily, too. Just by the patches a lot of the men citizens had on the back parts of their trousers, you could notice it.

"And so, when the Stellaland Republic started printing its own bank-notes, it looked as though everything would come right, then. But the affairs of the nation did not altogether follow out the course we expected. One thing was landladies of boarding-houses, I remember. What they wanted at the end of the month, they said, was, I remember very clearly, money. I don't think I have ever in my life, either before or since, heard quite that same kind of sniff. I mean, the kind of sniff a Stellaland Republic landlady would give at the end of the month if she saw you feeling in an envelope for bank-notes.

"Then there was the Indian storekeeper.

"I was with my friend, Giel Haasbroek, in the Indian store, and I'll never forget the look that came over the Indian's face when Giel Haasbroek produced a handful of Stellaland Republic bank-notes to pay him with. Amongst other things, what the Indian said was that he had a living to make, just like all of us.

"'But these notes are perfectly good,' Giel Haasbroek said to the Indian. 'Look, there's the picture of the Republic eagle across the top, here. And here, underneath, you can read for yourself the printed signatures of the President and the Minister of Finance — signed with their own hands, too.'

"I'll never forget how the Indian storekeeper winced, then, either. And the Indian said he had nothing against the eagle. He was willing to admit that it was the best kind of eagle that there was. He wouldn't argue about that. From where he came from, they didn't have eagles. And if you were to show him a whole lot of eagles in a row, he didn't think he would be able to tell the one from the other, hardly, the Indian said. We must not misunderstand him on that point, the Indian took pains to make clear to us. He had no intention of hurting our feelings in any way.

"But when it came to the signatures of the President and the Minister of Finance, then it was quite a different matter, the Indian said. For he had both their signatures in black and white for old debts that he knew he would never be able to collect, the Indian said. And of the two, the President was worse than the Minister of Finance, even. The President had got so, the Indian said, that for months, now, on his way to work in the morning, he would walk three blocks out of his way, round the other side of the plein, just so that he didn't have to pass the Indian's store."

Oupa Bekker interrupted his story to get a match from the school-teacher. That gave us a chance to ponder over what he had said. For they had fallen strangely on our ears, some of his words. There appeared to have been a certain starkness about the texture of life in the old days that our present-day imaginings could not too readily embrace.

"But they never caught on, really, those Stellaland Republic bank-notes," Oupa Bekker continued. "Afterwards the government withdrew the old bank-notes and brought out a new issue. But even that didn't help very much, I don't think. Although I must say that the new series of banknotes looked much nicer. The new bank-notes were bigger, for one thing. And they were printed in more colours than the old ones were. And they had a new kind of an eagle on the top. The eagle seemed more imposing, somehow. And he also had a threatening kind of look, that you couldn't miss. It was like the Stellaland Republic threatening you, if you got tendered one of those notes for board and lodging, and you were hesitating about taking it.

"But, all the same, those bank-notes never really seemed to circulate, very much. Maybe that Indian storekeeper was right in what he said. Perhaps after all it wasn't the eagle, so much, that they should have changed, as those two signatures on the lower portion of the banknote. Perhaps they should have been signed so that you couldn't read them.

"And, as I have said, the queer thing is that there was nothing wrong with those Stellaland Republic bank-notes. They weren't counterfeit notes in any way, I mean. They were absolutely legal. The eagle and the printing were both all right — they were the smartest-looking eagle and the smartest printing that you could get in those days. And yet — there you were."

We agreed with Oupa Bekker that the problem of money was pretty mixed up, and always had been. Shortly afterwards the

Government lorry arrived from Bekkersdal. The lorry-driver's assistant went up to the counter. "Change this fiver for me, please, Jurie," he said.

This was Jurie Steyn's turn to be funny. He took full advantage of it. He turned the note over several times.

"The printing looks all right," Jurie Steyn said. "And for all I know, the spelling is also all right. And the lion hasn't got a pipe in his mouth. What kind of a fool do you think I am — handing me a note like this? . . . About the only thing it hasn't got on it is an eagle."

Since he didn't know what our talk had been about, the lorry-driver's assistant looked only mystified.

WEATHER PROPHET

THAT was after At Naudé had gone over the whole thing several times, telling us not only what he had heard over the wireless, but also what he had read in the newspapers. He made it clear to us what a weather wizard was. He also explained — although in this case not quite so clearly, perhaps — the functions and *raison d'etre* of the meteorologist.

What made it more difficult for At Naudé was the fact that, while we already knew about weather prophecy, having met some prophets and having on occasion tried our hand at forecasting, ourselves — in time of sowing, say — the lengthy word, meteorologist, was a new one on us.

"All the same," Jurie Steyn persisted, after At Naudé had finished with his explanations, "I still don't see why you should speak in such an off-hand way about a weather prophet, just because he can prophesy a good while beforehand what the weather is going to be — and he gets it right. It shouldn't matter that he goes by just simple things like it's the last quarter of the moon on Wednesday and the wind changed last night."

Chris Welman expressed his agreement with Jurie Steyn.

"Well, I don't pretend to be a weather prophet or anything like," Chris Welman said, "but you'll remember how only last year I was right when I said, that time, that we'd have rain in three days. And when I said it there wasn't a cloud in the sky. But I just went by what my grandfather once said about when the wind blows from the Pilansberg with the new moon, what to expect."

And we said, yes, you could also tell if it was going to rain by other signs. "By the way swallows fly," Johnny Coen said. "And red ants walking around after sunset," Jurie Steyn said. "And by how the smoke comes out of the chimney," Gysbert van Tonder said. "And by spiders Oupa Bekker began.

At Naudé looked very superior, then, and he wore a thin smile.

"But you haven't any of you perhaps got a balloon going up on an island in the sea, have you?" he asked. "Or has any of you got a whole string of weather stations right through the Union? Just one weather station, even, maybe?"

With none of us answering, At Naudé looked more satisfied than ever with himself, then.

"That's where a meteorologist is different" At Naudé announced. "A meteorologist has got all those things." Although he realised then that he was beaten, Jurie Steyn could nevertheless not bring himself to yield straight away.

"It still doesn't make sense, quite," Jurie Steyn declared — but with less conviction than before — "that what you call a meteorologist doesn't say that next week there's going to be snow — and there is snow. Or that there is going to be a whirlwind — and then next week we've got no roofs left. It looks like it's only a weather prophet that comes and forecasts about that kind of thing. It looks like a meteorologist doesn't worry about it — or know of it, even."

"And does a meteorologist need to?" At Naudé asked, triumphantly. "Why should he trouble about working out when it's going to rain, say, seeing how he's got all those things for taking ground temperatures with, and for measuring the wind with, and he's got a balloon on an island in the sea? I mean, he's a scientist, a meteorologist is. You don't catch him walking outside to see what kind of smoke is coming out of his weather-station chimney. Or going by red ants — no matter how many red ants may be walking around after supper-time. Or by spiders—" The absurdity of that last idea struck At Naudé so forcibly that he spluttered. We laughed a little ourselves, too, then. Yes, bringing in spiders seemed to be going just too far.

"After all, a meteorologist must be a man with a certain amount of learning," At Naudé finished up. "And so, I don't suppose he'd be able to prophesy the weather right, even if he tried."

We could not but acknowledge, then, that what At Naudé said

was indeed true. Such weather prophets as we knew to speak to were not people of great learning. And when one of ourselves, for instance, forecast correctly about did we have to put a bucksail over the wagon on the road to Bekkersdal, then we realised, also, that our way of working it out did not owe much to the letters we had been taught to write on our slates in the school-room. It was easy to see that a meteorologist would be far above a thing just like telling us when to put in autumn giant cauliflowers. Our Hollander schoolmaster had been just as far above it, too.

"Of course, what helps you a lot in weather prophesying," Chris Welman said, "is mealies. I mean, after you've sown a patch of mealies, and they start coming up, then you know right away there's going to be a long piece of just absolute drought. And when a mealie gets to that size — if he ever gets to that size, I mean — where a head starts forming and you've got to have rain, then, or you won't get a crop at all, well, then you can be sure that for a whole month there's going to be just clear blue skies, so that you sit on your front stoep for day after day, working out in one of your children's school writing books how much you owe the Indian store-keeper at Ramoutsa.

"And when I see by my youngest son, Petrus's, quarterly report that he is good at sums, I think, yes, and I know what he's going to use all those sums for, one day, sitting on his front stoep with a pencil and a piece of paper, waiting for the rain. He'll need all the sums and more that they can teach him at school, I think to myself, then."

Thereupon Jurie Steyn, who was not unacquainted with conditions prevailing years ago in the Cape Zwartland, said that if there was anything better than a mealie for prophesying the weather with, it was just a wheat plant.

"When a wheat plant," Jurie Steyn continued, "has got to there where you say to yourself that next week you'll start reaping and so you've got to see about getting all the sickles sharpened, then it's almost as though that wheat plant is himself so educated that he can tell you not to worry about it. For there's going to be the biggest hailstorm in years — it's like it's the wheat plant himself that's telling you that: an ordinary Hard-Red wheat plant with no learning to speak of."

When it was a matter of hail, now, Oupa Bekker said, well, there was Klaas Rasmus. As a weather wizard, Klaas Rasmus could have been said to specialise in hail, Oupa Bekker explained. Of course, nobody knew what methods Klaas Rasmus employed, exactly, Oupa Bekker said, although it was reasonable to suppose that it wasn't weather charts and graphs and rainfall figures and things like that. For one thing, it was unlikely that Klaas Rasmus would have known what rainfall figures were if you showed them to him, even.

"Not that he would ever have let on that he didn't know," Oupa Bekker continued. "Klaas Rasmus was not that kind of a man at all. If you had shown him the kind of rainfall figures, say, that At Naudé has been talking about, Klaas Rasmus would have nodded his head up and down solemnly quite a number of times.

"And he would have said, yes, that was just about how he would have worked it out himself, he thought, if he had had a piece of paper handy with lines drawn on it like that, and all. And then he would ask were you sure you were holding those rainfall figures the right way up, seeing that there were just one or two things there that he wasn't sure if he agreed with, quite.

"You see, that was Klaas Rasmus all over. If he understood a thing or not, it didn't make much difference to him. He would have something to say about it, all the same. But because he was so good at prophesying hail (being proved right time and again) there were a lot of little weaknesses he had that we could over-look."

Jurie Steyn said, then, that he thought he had heard that name, Klaas Rasmus, before, somewhere. Didn't he have some sort of nickname, Jurie Steyn asked.

Yes, that was quite right, Oupa Bekker said. They used to call him Klaas Baksteen, because of the size of the hailstones that used to fall each time that he prophesied hail. The hail-stones would come down then the size of half bricks.

"And I also seem to remember from something that I heard of long ago," Jurie Steyn went on, "that he — No, I can't recall it quite, now. But it was something that didn't seem to make sense, altogether, in a way."

Oupa Bekker said that he believed he knew what it was that Jurie Steyn was thinking about — something that Jurie Steyn had been told, about a happening in the Marico long ago.

"You see, like with all cases of real greatness," Oupa Bekker said, "there was some doubt, in some people's minds, about whether Klaas Baksteen was really as good at prophesying hail as he was held to be. There was talk that he was wrong, sometimes. And there was also talk that he would only forecast that there was going to be hail the size of half-bricks when the sky was already black and high up, and with awful white patches just above the horizon from which a child of four would know that after another half an hour there would be no harvest left that year.

"And so, one day, when he had worked out, to the hour, almost, when there was going to be a hail-storm the like of which this part of the Marico had rarely seen, and that hailstorm still a week ahead, Klaas Baksteen journeyed down to Bekkersdal so that the editor of the newspaper there could print it in his newspaper well before the hail-storm actually happened. And Klaas Baksteen put up at an hotel there, deciding to wait until his prophecy came out. And they say that everybody was very interested, of course. And quite a lot of people who didn't believe in Klaas Baksteen's powers said that that would show him up, all right, seeing that his prophecy was printed in the newspaper.

"And they say that it must have been pretty dreadful for Klaas Baksteen himself, waiting there in that hotel on the day when there was to be the hail-storm — more especially since up to quite late in the afternoon it was an absolutely cloudless sky. And Klaas Baksteen worried about it so much that afterwards he sent for a brandy, even, to try and calm himself. And afterwards he sent for another brandy. And when the waiter brought him the second brandy the sunlight shining on the glass was so bright that it blinded Klaas Baksteen, almost. That was how little chance there seemed to be of hail, then."

Oupa Bekker put a match to his pipe and puffed steadily for some moments.

"But before it was evening," he said, "there was such a hail-storm in Bekkersdal that hardly a window was left unbroken. Well, that was a proud moment for Klaas Baksteen, all right. Just with that he proved that he was the greatest hail-prophet in the world. And before the sun had quite set a man who cultivated asparagus under glass frames just outside the town came and called on Klaas Baksteen at the hotel. And you've got no idea how proud Klaas Baksteen was that that man visited him. Even though Klaas Baksteen always used to wear a moustache after that. It was a thick, curling sort of moustache that Klaas Baksteen grew to cover up the place where his front teeth used to be before the asparagus man called round to see him."

But he couldn't understand that, Jurie Steyn said. It didn't make sense to him, Jurie Steyn said, quite. Although he had heard something about it, he seemed to remember.

"Well, why Klaas Baksteen was so happy about it," Oupa Bekker said, "was because that proved how great a weather prophet he was. The man who grew asparagus under glass frames proved it, by cutting up so rough. It made Klaas Baksteen king of hail-prophets, that."

MOTHER-IN-LAW

"IT'S not that she's here now," Jurie Steyn said. "Not actually in the house, I mean. Last time I saw her was about half an hour ago. She had her hat on."

So Chris Welman said that he could sympathise with Jurie Steyn, since having your mother-in-law coming to stay with you was about the oldest kind of trouble that there was in the world.

And he always used to think that with himself it would be different. For that reason, he had been, in the past, not a little impatient when other men had spoken about how much sorrow had come into their lives from that moment when they opened the top part of the front door and there was an elderly little lady standing there with suitcases.

"Looking as though butter wouldn't melt in her mouth," Jurie Steyn declared.

It was because those married men who spoke like that didn't have proper feelings, he used to think when he was first married, Chris Welman went on. And he used to think that a man must have a very mean heart if he didn't have room in it for a frail little old lady standing at the front door with —

"Not so frail little, either," Jurie Steyn interjected. "And with her hair fastened back in a tight bun. And sniffing suspiciously if there's a smell of drink, before she's got her foot right in over the front step."

He also used to think, Chris Welman continued, that if for no other reason than just for his wife's sake a man should be able to force himself to act in a kindly way towards his mother-in-law, no matter what he thought of her privately.

If he was anything of a man at all, that was, Chris Welman used to believe. And he never saw anything funny, either, in jokes about a mother-in-law. He used to shake his head in a pitying way when a man told what was to be a comic story about a mother-in-law.

"And her saying 'It's all right, there's nothing in that suitcase that can break,' while you're carrying it inside for her," Jurie Steyn said. "Trying to make out that it's through drink that you stumbled over a chair, when all the time it was because you were nervous."

But Chris Welman said that his own ideas underwent a considerable degree of modification as a result of his mother-in-law having come to pay them a somewhat extended visit.

"Now I come to think of it," Chris Welman remarked, "she didn't really stay very long. It only looked like that. And then when it came to the time when it was understood that she would be going back again, she at the last moment stretched out her stay. Once more, I must be honest and admit that she didn't stretch it out very much. And it wasn't through her own doing, either, that it happened like that. But people who knew me well, and whom I hadn't come across over that time, told me how much I had aged since they had last seen me.

"Anyway, why my mother-in-law stretched out her visit was because there was trouble with the Government lorry that she had to go back on. It took the lorry-driver and his assistant the best part of two hours to get the engine going again. And that was the length of time that my mother-in-law stretched out her visit. As I say, I don't claim it was her fault in any way. Although actually, I am not so sure, either. I mean, when I think of some of the things she did get up to—"

All the same, Chris Welman added, he even today couldn't see anything funny in mother-in-law jokes. He had noticed that that kind of joke was always told by a coarse type of person with no real feelings. Just let such a person have the experience of having his mother-in-law come and stay with him — just once, Chris Welman said — and that person would never laugh at a mother-in-law joke again. In fact, he doubted if that person would ever again in his life laugh at anything, very much.

53

"The worst thing," Jurie Steyn announced, "is the comparisons she makes. Not so much in words, either, perhaps, as in other ways. And by hints. How her other daughter that's married to the booking-office clerk has got coal to burn in her kitchen stove and hasn't got to go out with a Price's candles box to pick up cow-dung—"

"Not today she can't," At Naudé interjected. "Not with the coal shortage in the towns that the newspapers are full of. Today she'd be glad to have just that candles box to burn, if I know anything."

"Or the comparison she makes with her youngest son, Jebe-diah, who is now a deacon in the church," Jurie Steyn contin-ued. "Well, I'm not saying anything about Jebediah, the way he is today. Because I only knew Jebediah before he was a church deacon, and that was on the diggings. Well, the diggings would hardly be a place for a church deacon to feel at home on, especial-ly the kind of life that was led on the diggings in those days. But I'll say this much for Jebediah — that he never once let on how hard it was for him to fit into that low life, or what a nightmare it was to him. You would never imagine what a suffering it was for him to stay in that sinful place — the way he took to it, I mean.

"And I suppose Jebediah would still be there today, sitting in a saloon bar and doing his best to close his eyes to all the disgrace around him, if it wasn't that the diggers' committee afterwards called on him and ran him off the diggings. For some reason, while they were talking to him, the diggers' committee were also pouring tar on Jebediah, and they were shaking feathers on to Jebediah out of a pillow that they had brought along." And it was that same Jebediah, Jurie Steyn said, that his mother-in-law was today holding up to him as an example. Not always in so many words, perhaps, Jurie Steyn said, but certainly by way of hint and allusion.

"And if I try ever so slightly, and without mentioning anything near the worst, even," Jurie Steyn said, "to give her a perhaps dif-ferent idea of her Jebediah, then she just sits back and smiles. She acts like she feels sorry for me because she thinks I'm jealous of

Jebediah. What came out of that pillow-case seemed to be muscovy duck feathers, mostly."

It was pretty much that sort of thing in his own case, Chris Welman said, that led to so radical a change being effected in his outlook.

"I don't think I would have minded so much if it was just her son that my mother-in-law said was so much better than me, the time she came to stay with us," Chris Welman said. "I think I could have stood for that. In any case, I was at school with her son, and he used to copy spelling off me in class. And that used to make me feel very proud — to see him copying. Because until then I used to think that I was the worst at spelling in the whole school."

Later on, however, the schoolmaster was to declare openly that that other pupil (that nobody knew then would one day be Chris Welman's brother-in-law) was the worst at spelling in the whole of the schoolmaster's experience.

"And no one guessed," Chris Welman said, "that why he was so bad was because he was all the time copying off me. And so you can see that, no matter what his mother might say, I could never have anything against him. But it was her late husband that she would always talk about. That and—"

"Yes," Jurie Steyn remarked. "And drink."

"Because I would take a little mampoer brandy now and again to cheer myself up," Chris Welman continued, "she would act as though I was a miserable lost drunkard that regularly beat his wife black and blue. And I used to get to feeling that way about myself, too, that I was a lost miserable drunkard—"

Gysbert van Tonder interposed, then, with the comment that as far as he could see the visit of Chris Welman's mother-in-law could only have done good. There could have been no flies on her, Gysbert van Tonder said, for her to have been able to sum up so quickly what was Chris Welman's trouble. Although she would have been pretty unobservant if she hadn't noticed — the moment she stepped in at the front door, even. And that was all the thanks she got for it — with Chris Welman talking so ungratefully about her now, and all.

He only hoped, Gysbert van Tonder said, that Chris Welman didn't forget himself so far as to beat his mother-in-law black and blue as well. All the same, he added, he could quite understand, now, why that kindly old lady's visit should have upset Chris Welman so much, seeing that she just meant everything for the best. It was through no fault of hers that Chris Welman was what he was.

"If you had taken her reproof to heart more," Gysbert van Tonder said, "you would have been a different man today. Instead of being just hardened in your awful habits and not being able to find a good word to say about your own wife's mother. And all that goes for Jurie Steyn, too."

Before the two personages so addressed could think of a suitable reply, At Naudé mentioned that he had that same afternoon seen Jurie Steyn's mother-in-law. She was walking across the veld. Walking at a good pace, At Naudé said.

"Yes, I've already told you that I saw her put her hat on and go out," Jurie Steyn said. But he added that he was not going to be foolishly hopeful about it, seeing that she hadn't taken her suitcases with her.

"About her late husband, now," Chris Welman said, reverting to the subject of his own mother-in-law. "It was when she stood looking at the front of the house that she said that was where her late husband was different, now. Her late husband would never have allowed the front of his house to get so dilapidated, she said. Not even when he had got so with the rheumatics that sometimes he wouldn't show his face outside of his bedroom for days on end. You see, in those days they used to call it rheumatics. Well, any way, it was for that reason that I got out the old stepladder and a bucket of whitewash and started on the front of my house.

"And then, of course, my mother-in-law had to come past and say that one thing about her late husband was that he would never splash the whitewash on just anyhow, but that he would apply it with even strokes of the brush and not get his face and the brush-handle and his clothes all messed up.

"And then when the string of the step-ladder broke on account of its being so old, she didn't even ask me did I get hurt falling, or could she help me get my foot out of the whitewash bucket. She just said that her late husband would never have got on to a step-ladder drunk and then have tried to murder her from there."

So Gysbert van Tonder said, well, what did Chris Welman expect? If Chris Welman got on to a step-ladder with a bucket of whitewash and he was full of mampoer, there would be almost bound to be trouble, Gysbert van Tonder said.

"I've already told you it was the string," Chris Welman answered, sounding surly. "In any case, during all the time that my mother-in-law stayed with us I never once had a drink in the house. Before my mother-in-law came, I moved the brandy still out of the wagon-house and went and hid it in an old potato shed in the kloof that I didn't use any more because it was too far out of the way. That was where I used to go when I needed a drink, then — all that far."

Gysbert van Tonder made a clicking sort of sound, to show how upset he was at the thought that a man could be so degraded. The way he was carrying on, it looked as though it was Gysbert van Tonder and not Jurie Steyn's brother-in-law, Jebediah, that was the church deacon.

"And what I'll never forget," Chris Welman proceeded, "is that afternoon when my cattle herd, 'Mbulu, came running to tell me that the old miesies had come to him in the veld and had sent him to fetch the police at Nietverdiend. But 'Mbulu didn't go for the police, of course. He knew better than that. He came and fetched me instead. I hurried along with him and he led me straight to where my mother-in-law was standing right in front of the disused potato shed. 'It's too terrible,' she said when I arrived. 'I only hope the police get here in time. Do you know what's inside this shed? No, I'm sure you'll never guess. It's a still. It means that the Bechuanas on your farm are making brandy here in secret. If you stand here and look through this crack in the door you can see it's a still.'

"I pretended to look, of course, and I said, yes, she was right, and it was too terrible to think of how out of hand the Bechuanas were getting. I would talk to them about it very severely, I said, seeing that what they were doing was so low and illegal, and all. But, of course, we mustn't bring the police into it, I said. We didn't want that kind of trouble on the farm. But you've got no idea how hard it was to dissuade my mother-in-law, who had worked it out that the sergeant from Nietverdiend could get there in under an hour.

"In the end I was actually pleading with her to give those shameless Bechuanas another chance: even if (as she said) their making illicit mampoer brandy was worse than if they had still been cannibals. Afterwards she relented. But it was only after I had satisfied her that I had broken every jar in the potato shed and there was nothing left of the still but a few yards of twisted brass tubing that you could never put together again."

Chris Welman sighed. "And to think that it was one of the finest brandy stills in the whole of the Groot Marico," he said, finally.

Jurie Steyn was looking strangely agitated.

"But where did you say she was going," he asked of At Naudé, "walking over the veld with her hat on? I mean, what *direction* did she take? Talk quick, man."

At Naudé explained to the best of his ability.

"Oh," Jurie Steyn ejaculated. "Oh, my God."

THE TERROR OF THE MALOPO

OUPA Bekker was camped out near Renosterpoort with Japie Uys on an afternoon of long ago when a stranger who was tall and dark came riding up to them from out of the bush. That was how he met Hubrecht Willemse, Oupa Bekker said to us.

"I didn't know the man who dismounted there where Japie Uys and I were resting," Oupa Bekker explained. "But I knew his horse. It was one of Koos Liebenberg's prize stallions. I also knew the saddle. It belonged to Gert Pretorius. And the suit the stranger had on was Krisjan Steyn's black church-clothes."

Oupa Bekker said that he identified the suit by the mended place in the knee of the trousers from where Krisjan Steyn fell on the sidewalk in front of the Zeerust bar one Nagmaal. Why Krisjan Steyn fell was because of the half-dozen steps in front of the bar that he hadn't noticed on account of the heat.

"The stranger introduced himself as Hubrecht Willemse," Oupa Bekker added, "and he said he had been round the neighbourhood a bit. Well, a good bit, he could have said, I thought judging from his suit and horse, not to mention Gert Pretorius's saddle.

"Japie Uys and I looked at each other. And I was glad I wasn't Japie. For Japie Uys was wearing a new pair of store boots that would be just about the stranger's size."

Oupa Bekker said that Hubrecht Willemse came and sat down on a fallen tree-trunk beside Japie Uys and himself.

Hubrecht Willemse took off his hat and fanned himself with it.

"And I don't know whose hat it was," Oupa Bekker said, "although it looked so old and shapeless that I wouldn't be surprised if it was Hubrecht Willemse's own hat.

"But it was when we saw how short Hubrecht Willemse's hair had been cut that Japie Uys started apologising very fast for the uncomfortable tree-stump that Hubrecht Willemse had to sit on. There was a much better trunk he knew of just down the road, Japie Uys said, and he was already half-way disappearing into a clump of withaaks after it, when Hubrecht Willemse called him back pretty sharply.

"'None of that,' Hubrecht Willemse said when Japie Uys returned, looking sheepish. 'You're going to stay right here, both of you.'"

Oupa Bekker said that although it was a hot afternoon, yet, sitting there in the bush next to Hubrecht Willemse on a fallen tree-trunk, he actually found himself shivering. He didn't feel very different from a hollowed-out tree-trunk himself, Oupa Bekker said.

Then there was a sudden, cracking sound. The white ants had been at work in the inside of that tree-trunk, and so the wood gave way in one place, with the weight of three men on it. Nevertheless, both Oupa Bekker and Japie Uys jumped.

"When we sat down again," Oupa Bekker proceeded, "Hubrecht Willemse said to us, 'You know, I'm an escaped convict.' Just like that, he said it. Of course, that information did not come as much of a surprise to Japie Uys and myself. All the same, we thought that the stranger might feel better about it if we pretended to be astonished.

"So Japie Uys said, no, he just couldn't believe it. It was just about the last thing he would have imagined, Japie Uys assured Hubrecht Willemse. And I said to him that I thought he looked more like an insurance agent.

"Then remembering about a bit of unpleasantness that there had been with an insurance agent in those parts not so long ago, I said he looked more like a Senator, perhaps."

Oupa Bekker said that his words did not please Hubrecht Willemse as much as he thought they might.

"But it was Hubrecht Willemse's next remark that made me

wonder if he was quite right in the head," Oupa Bekker continued. "I started thinking that the years he had spent behind prison walls, with just rice-water and singing hymns, must have turned his mind queer. I got a chillier feeling than ever between my shoulder-blades, then, in spite of the heat."

For Hubrecht Willemse told Oupa Bekker that the reason why the men from the landdrost's office would not be able to capture him was because he had the power to render himself invisible.

"Sometimes they don't see me at all," Hubrecht Willemse said to Oupa Bekker. "Other times they think I'm somebody else. I've noticed it all the way through these parts. That's why I am glad that I'll be crossing the border soon.

"Because it's worrying me a bit, this thing. It's a power I didn't have before. It must be something that came to me without my knowing about it, this last time I was in prison. Maybe it was something I ate."

Oupa Bekker said that he thought to himself, then, that it was not so very surprising that the landdrost's men should make mistakes about Hubrecht Willemse's identity.

"I thought, well, if I had seen him from not so very near by," Oupa Bekker said, "and I went just by the horse he was riding, then I might easily have taken him for Koos Liebenberg. Or, again, if I had seen him just walking, with the light not too good, and going by how he was dressed, then I might have thought he was Krisjan Steyn.

"So it was not so surprising that the landdrost's men, who did not have occasion to visit the Dwarsberg side of the Groot Marico often, should get a bit mixed-up, perhaps, in looking for Hubrecht Willemse. Like if he should walk into a bar, for instance, carrying Gert Pretorius's saddle under his arm, I also thought."

In the meantime, Oupa Bekker said, Japie Uys had been sitting in an absent-minded way kicking at small pieces of leiklip in front of the stump.

"That's not the way to treat store boots," Hubrecht Willemse informed Japie Uys gruffly. "I can see they're good boots — almost new, by the look of them. But they won't look like that much longer, the way you're going on. What did you say your name was? Swanepoel?"

Oupa Bekker said he wondered if the stranger had been to Welgevonden, also. "No," Japie Uys said, "my name is Uys. Japie Uys. But I don't mind if you would prefer to call me by some other name. It doesn't make any difference to me at all, really. You can just go on calling me Swanepoel, if you want."

"Well, look here, Uys," Hubrecht Willemse said. "That's not the thing to do — kicking stones around with store boots. If you want to kick stones, take your boots off, first, and kick the stones barefoot."

But Japie Uys said that he didn't really want to kick stones. He was doing it just without thinking, Japie Uys said.

Japie Uys went on to explain that why he was wearing his new boots at all, out on the veld like that, was because they were a bit tight and he wanted to walk them in. They still hurt him in a few places, he said, still.

"Where do they hurt you?" Hubrecht Willemse demanded.

Japie Uys said, well, in his feet, mostly.

"Well, they couldn't very well hurt you in your back, could they?" Hubrecht Willemse burst out. "What part of your feet do your boots — I mean, those boots — still pinch?"

Japie Uys told him.

Oupa Bekker said that what went on during the next hour or so was most inhuman to watch. The way Hubrecht Willemse made Japie Uys walk and stamp and prance around on the most uneven pieces of ground he could find, Japie Uys having to take particular care that the uppers of the boots did not get scratched by wag-'n-bietjie thorns, and Hubrecht Willemse calling Japie Potgieter, all the time.

"Afterwards, when Hubrecht Willemse rode off, wearing Japie Uys's boots and leaving his own worn veldskoens behind," Oupa Bekker said, "Japie Uys, with his exhaustion and sore feet, was about the most suffering-looking white man I had ever seen.

"And the awful time he had gone through made him do quite a strange thing. For the moment Hubrecht Willemse had galloped out of sight Japie Uys rose up and took a flying kick, with his bare foot, at a piece of leiklip."

Japie Uys collapsed forward on to his face, then, Oupa Bekker, said, and he didn't move again until about sunset. And what Japie Uys said about Hubrecht Willemse then, Oupa Bekker added, was most unchristian.

It was next day, Oupa Bekker said, that he saw for himself something of that mysterious power that Hubrecht Willemse spoke about having, whereby Hubrecht Willemse could become invisible or could appear to be somebody quite different.

"We were again sitting on that tree-stump," Oupa Bekker said, "Japie Uys having his feet wrapped in pieces of sacking that we had in the mule-cart. And Japie Uys was talking a good deal about Hubrecht Willemse, mostly about what he would like to do to him."

A horseman again drew up in front of them, Oupa Bekker said, and came and joined them on the tree-stump. But this time they recognised the visitor. It was the veldkornet, who had been sent from the landdrost's office on the escaped convict's trail.

"Japie Uys and I were both very glad to see the veldkornet," Oupa Bekker said, "and the veldkornet was able to tell us a lot about Hubrecht Willemse, whom he described as a dangerous character. But we knew that much without the veldkornet telling us. 'Whatever he wants he just takes, and he doesn't care how,' the veldkornet said. That, too, we knew."

The veldkornet went on to say that in the records of the landdrost's office Hubrecht Willemse was known as the Terror of the Malopo.

"What, has he been there as well?" Japie Uys said.

"No," the veldkornet replied, "but that's where he's headed for. And if he's not going to be a holy terror there, in the Malopo, then

I don't know. But it's outside our district, and the quicker he gets there, the better we'll all like it, I can tell you."

Oupa Bekker said that he thought that was a very peculiar way for a veldkornet to talk. Never mind about wanting to call Hubrecht Willemse the Terror of the Malopo, Oupa Bekker thought, why, he was enough of a Terror of the Marico. Oupa Bekker tried to suggest something along those lines to the veldkornet.

"Well, if he gets into the Malopo, then it's their lookout," was all the veldkornet would say.

The veldkornet wasn't even much interested, Oupa Bekker said, in the veldskoens that Hubrecht Willemse had left behind, and to which Japie Uys directed the veldkornet's attention, saying that if the veldkornet smelt them, it might help to put him on the trail of the escaped convict.

"But the veldkornet said that wouldn't help much," Oupa Bekker went on. "When once Hubrecht Willemse had got across the Malopo, it wasn't so very far from there to the Bechuanaland border. Yes, he wouldn't be at all surprised if Hubrecht Willemse was almost out of the Transvaal by now."

Oupa Bekker said that, in spite of his feet, Japie Uys laughed, then. You couldn't get to the Bechuanaland border that way, Japie Uys said. Not at that time of the year, you couldn't. The only way was through the Renosterpoort. And from where he was sitting on the stump, Japie Uys pointed out the Renosterpoort to the veldkornet.

"That scoundrel Willemse will have to come right back here, again, along that same road," Japie Uys said, gleefully. "He'll have to. There's no other way. And that's when you'll get him. The blisters and skinned places on my feet don't feel quite so sore, now. What's more, Hubrecht Willemse will be coming past here again, quite soon."

Just then another cracking sound came from the hollowed-out tree-trunk. This time it was the veldkornet that jumped up suddenly, Oupa Bekker said.

"And later on, that same afternoon it was proved to us that Hubrecht Willemse did have those ghostly powers that he claimed," Oupa Bekker added. "For Hubrecht Willemse came back again along that road, as Japie Uys had said he would. And from a long way off we pointed him out to the veldkornet. But the veldkornet just couldn't see him at all.

"And when, afterwards, Hubrecht Willemse got so near that the veldkornet just had to see him, the veldkornet said that it didn't look like Hubrecht Willemse to him in the least.

"It looked more like a Senator he knew, the veldkornet re-marked when Hubrecht Willemse had gone past, and the sound of galloping hooves was dying in the distance."

FEAT OF MEMORY

"WHERE'S that rubber stamp, now?" Jurie Steyn said, letting his eye travel the length of his post-office counter. "I'm sure I had it here a few minutes ago. Right in my hand I had it."

"What's that thing you've still got in your hand, there, Jurie?" Chris Welman asked.

So Jurie Steyn said, well, if that didn't beat everything.

"If I didn't see it happening myself, right with my own eyes, I wouldn't believe it possible that a man could be so forgetful," Jurie Steyn said. "It's trouble does that to a person, of course, making him absent-minded like that — trouble and a high kind of official responsibility."

There were a few things that we would have all liked to have said about that, of course. We would have liked to have made mention of some of the quite unusual sorts of mistakes that happened in the post office, sometimes, with letters and parcels. And it would have given us pleasure, too, to have said that, everything considered, it was not surprising that errors of a kind we could mention crept into certain aspects of the post office's functionings. If there were other post-office servants with Jurie Steyn's high sense of official responsibility, we would have liked to have said. Instead, we let it pass. There were certain things, we knew, that Jurie Steyn did not like to be rubbed up the wrong way about.

The only one of us to make any comment at all was Gysbert van Tonder. And Gysbert contented himself with a mild statement to the effect that, with the way things were today, when you rolled up the sleeve of your right arm in order to sit down and pen a letter, you were taking your life into your own hands.

"Anyway, it said over the wireless the other night," At Naudé remarked somewhat hurriedly — in order to forestall unpleasantness, maybe — "that some of the greatest men in history have also had some of the worst memories. And it wasn't only learned men, like professors (that we all know have got very bad memories) that were like that. But also men without any kind of learning at all — men like great politicians, for instance, it said over the wireless."

And also, of the men in history with poor memories that hadn't had much learning, At Naudé continued, were some of the world's great educators. Some of the world's greatest writers of textbooks for high-school use, the wireless said.

So Jurie Steyn said, well, of course, he had never put forward any claims himself to having an outstanding memory. In fact, even with his job as postmaster he made mistakes, sometimes, through forgetting things, that he was sure would afford us a great deal of amusement one day when he had time to go into it all. Like he would sometimes forget for weeks on end to send a registered package on. It was really awfully funny, Jurie Steyn said.

Thereupon Gysbert van Tonder made mention of a number of great politicians that he had known in his time who suffered from extraordinary lapses of memory. There was one politician in particular, Gysbert van Tonder said, who, when he came round to the Marico before an election, knew every farmer by his first name and knew the ages of each of the farmer's children and knew where each child came in class at the end of the term. And yet, because of that high kind of official responsibility that Jurie Steyn had mentioned, the politician's memory just went completely, immediately after he had been elected.

"And when I went to see him in Pretoria, he hardly knew who I was, even," Gysbert van Tonder said. "But for that I could perhaps not blame him so much, seeing that I hardly knew who he was, either, with that dark suit he was wearing, like a manel, and with a high, stick-up collar. And when I put my hand in my pocket and he saw that what I pulled out was only my tobacco pouch, a disappointed look came over his face that remained there right through all the time I had that interview with him.

"But how I saw that his memory had got really bad was when I mentioned a small favour that he had promised to do me. He had made me that promise sitting in my own voorkamer, even, drinking coffee. And yet when I spoke to him in Pretoria he had no recollection of ever having been in my voorkamer. And as for the coffee, he said he had drunk so much bad coffee in the Marico that he would actually be glad to forget that part."

Talking about that kind of thing (Oupa Bekker remarked at this stage), well, the man with the most extraordinary powers of memory that he had ever come across in the whole of the lowveld was Sarel Meintjies — "Rooi" Sarel, they called him, from the colour of his hair. And there was nothing "Rooi" Sarel ever forgot, Oupa Bekker said. But just nothing.

"Except perhaps one thing, only," Oupa Bekker continued, reflectively. "Or, at least, that was how it seemed to some of us afterwards. But if people were talking, say, like the way we're talking in Jurie Steyn's voorkamer, now, "Rooi" Sarel would remember years afterwards, even, exactly what each one said. And dates — and figures — why, you've got no idea. If you asked him, for instance, when was the big anthrax outbreak, he could tell you exactly to the year and month.

"And he could tell you in numbers what losses each farmer in the Dwarsberg area suffered, and how much each one got paid out by the Government in compensation. And he could also inform you precisely how long Japie Krige got for it, afterwards, when the Government found out just how wrong the figures were that Japie Krige had filled in in his compensation form.

"Or if you asked him how many years ago it was that the post-cart got overturned at the Malopo drift, when the driver was sacked for it, because the authorities thought he had capsized the post-cart on purpose and not just because of an illness that he was taking peach brandy for — why, then, "Rooi" Sarel would be able to acquaint you with it to the day, and almost to the exact hour, even. And it wasn't just because it was "Rooi" Sarel himself that was the driver of that post-cart that it was possible for him to remember so well. If it was somebody else that had been the driver of the post-cart and that was sacked for upsetting it, "Rooi" Sarel would have had all the facts at his finger-tips just the same.

"Or if you took "Rooi" Sarel once along a road, for instance, he would never afterwards forget that road. And if you turned right off from the road and went through the veld, even, and no matter how far, it was something that made you feel you wanted to laugh your head off at it, almost, afterwards, when you found out how faithfully "Rooi" Sarel could recall every inch of the way you took."

When Oupa Bekker paused to refill his pipe, Johnny Coen expressed the opinion that it must be of considerable advantage to a man to be blessed with gifts of an order such as Oupa Bekker credited "Rooi" Sarel with. He himself did not have a particularly retentive mind, Johnny Coen confessed, and what served to make it even worse, actually, he found, was that in recalling past circumstances and events he would as likely as not remember a lot of things also that never happened. To have that kind of a mind was, in a way, more of a handicap to a man than to have that other kind of a mind, where you simply forgot whole stretches of incidents.

More than once, Johnny Coen said, he had through this mental peculiarity of his been placed in an embarrassing situation — like seeming to remember that a girl in a blue dress and a white hat and shoes had smiled at him once when there was a Nagmaal. And then that girl's young man had come and made it clear to him, later on, about how his memory had deceived him. One reason why he agreed so readily that he had been mistaken, Johnny Coen added, was because the girl in the blue dress's young man was a weight-lifter, and had medals for it.

"It is on that account," Johnny Coen said, "that I have so much respect for that man, "Rooi" Sarel, that Oupa Bekker has told us about. I am sure that "Rooi" Sarel would never have made an ignorant mistake like what I made. He would have recalled right away that the weight-lifter's girl had not even looked at him. And a man like "Rooi" Sarel, with those great gifts of his for remembering things — well, I feel he must have been very proud to have been able to make use of his gifts to help other people. I mean, not only the Marico district, but the whole country — all the nation, that is — would be benefited through having in its midst somebody with such fine powers of memory as "Rooi" Sarel's, put to their proper use. Even if "Rooi" Sarel did not get rewarded for it in the way he should have been, perhaps."

Oupa Bekker, having got his pipe to draw satisfactorily again — satisfactorily for himself, that was, it being a matter of lesser importance that the young schoolmaster, seated next to Oupa Bekker, had started coughing — said that he would not argue with Johnny Coen. For it was indeed a truth that "Rooi" Sarel had been able to place his unusual talents at the disposal of the nation. And it was also true that in terms of hard cash he had not been over-generously rewarded. And yet there were those among the farmers of the Groot Marico who felt that "Rooi" Sarel's abilities could have been more commendably employed.

"As I have said," Oupa Bekker continued, "it was "Rooi" Sarel driving the post-cart when it capsized at the Malopo drift. And you can imagine how he must have looked when he crawled out of the water. And because all the other farmers around there had their hands full with their own troubles — since it was then right in the middle of the anthrax outbreak, and even though the government was talking about paying the farmers compensation, it was uncertain as to how much it was going to be — nobody was able to give much thought to the misfortune that "Rooi" Sarel was in — climbing out of the drift with the sack, and with his clothes wringing wet.

"In the end it was Japie Krige, with quite a few misfortunes of his own, at the time, that took "Rooi" Sarel in, feeding and clothing him and giving him enough money to get to Pretoria and to keep him there until he found work again.

"And then, afterwards, as you know, there was that scandal about the compensations. It got to the ears of the authorities that some of the farmers had received money for losses they had never suffered. And that was when the police started offering rewards to people who could say — who could prove, that is, you know — who could —"

"Who could give evidence leading to the arrest and conviction of party/parties aforementioned in sub-section 2 (a)," young Vermaak, the schoolmaster said, having stopped coughing by then.

"That was where "Rooi" Sarel's great powers of memory stood him in such good stead," Oupa Bekker continued, "even though he had not stayed at Japie Krige's farm very long, and even though the reward offered by the police was not really very large.

"But there were some farmers in these parts who said that, with his remarkable memory and all, there was one thing that "Rooi" Sarel forgot. It was a pity they said, that with so many things that he was able to remember, he should have forgotten where his loyalty lay."

MAN TO MAN

THE young mounted policeman, Bothma, explained of course, that why he had called round at Jurie Steyn's post office, that afternoon, was just because he was on his regular rounds. He hadn't picked that afternoon, particularly, he added. And he hadn't come to Jurie Steyn's post office specially, any more than he would visit any other post office or voorkamer in that part of the Groot Marico specially, he said.

It was only that he was carrying out his duties of patrolling the area, he explained, and it just so happened that in the course of routine he was patrolling over Jurie Steyn's farm, then.

He was new to the job of being a mounted policeman, young Bothma added.

Well, we realised that much about him, of course, without his having had to say it. And because he was new to his work, we made a good deal of allowance for him. But we were also pretty sure that the time would come when Mounted Constable Bothma would learn a few more things.

And he would understand then that nothing could rouse people's suspicions more than that a policeman should come round and offer all sorts of excuses for his being there.

"I just sort of make a few notes in my notebook," Bothma went on, "to say at what time, and so on, I call at each farmhouse that I do call on, patrolling, like I said."

Gysbert van Tonder yawned.

You could see, from the policeman's taking out his notebook and pencil like that, right at the beginning of his visit, and before he had sat down properly, almost, that he would yet have a long way to go and would have to traverse many a mile of made bushveld road and bridle path, asking a multitude of questions and getting the same number of wrong answers, before his call at an isolated farmhouse would make the farmer start thinking quickly to himself.

But the way Bothma was now, the farmer wouldn't ask him had he come through the vlakte — expecting the policeman to say, untruthfully, no, he had followed the government road as far as the poort. The farmer's thoughts would not travel with lightning speed to his brandy still. Nor would the farmer wonder if those few head of Bechuana cattle were safe in the truck to the Johannesburg market.

All those things we could sense about Constable Bothma in Jurie Steyn's voorkamer that afternoon. It was also apparent to us that, before arriving at where we were, he had called on more than one bushveld farmer en route. That would account for something of the diffidence in his manner. It was easy to guess that he had asked a few stock questions along the road — not that there was anything specific that he wanted to know, really, as he would no doubt have explained, but just because asking those questions was a part of his patrol duties — and it was only reasonable to suppose that the answers some of the Marico farmers had given him were not characterised by a noteworthy degree of artlessness.

He had doubtless discovered that while a policeman's questions might be, in terms of standing orders, stereotyped, a farmer's replies, generally speaking, weren't. Especially when that farmer's answers were being written straight into a notebook.

Nevertheless, because Bothma was, after all, a mounted policeman and in khaki uniform, with brass letters on his shoulders, we did feel a measure of constraint in his company. This circumstance of our not feeling quite at ease manifested itself in the way that most of us sat on our riempies-chairs — just a little more stiffly than usual, our shoulders not quite touching the backs of the chairs. It also manifested itself in the unconventional way in which Gysbert van Tonder saw fit to sprawl in his seat, in an affectation of a mental content that would have awakened mistrustful imaginings in the breast of a policeman who had been, say, two and a half years at the game.

It was then that Chris Welman made a remark that went a good way towards relieving the tension. Afterwards, in talking it over, we had to say that we could not but admire the manner in which Chris Welman had worked out the right words to use. Not that there was anything clever in the way that Chris Welman spoke, of course.

No, we all felt that the statement Chris Welman made then was something that was easily within the capacity of any one of us, if we had just sat back a little, and thought, and had then made use of the common-sense that comes to anybody that has lived on a farm long enough.

"The man you should really ask questions of," Chris Welman said to Constable Bothma, "is Gysbert van Tonder. That's him there. Sitting with his legs taking up half the floor and his hands behind his head, with his elbows stretched out. Just from the way he's sitting, you can see he's the biggest cattle-smuggler in the whole of the Dwarsberg area."

Well, that gave us a good laugh, of course. We all knew that Gysbert van Tender smuggled more cattle across the Konventie border than any other man in the Marico. What was more, we knew that Gysbert van Tonder's father had been regularly bringing in cattle over the line from Ramoutsa before there had ever been a proper barbed-wire fence there, even. And we also knew that, in the long years of the future, when we were all dead and gone, Gysbert van Tonder's sons would still be doing the same thing.

What was more, nothing would ever stop them, either. And not even if every policeman from Cape Town to the Limpopo knew about it. For the Bechuanas from whom he traded cattle felt friendly towards Gysbert van Tonder. And that was a sentiment they did not have for a border policeman, unreasonable though such an attitude of mind might perhaps seem. Moreover, this was an outlook on life, that, to a not inconsiderable degree, Gysbert van Tonder shared with the Bechuanas.

Consequently, in having spoken in the way he did, Chris Welman had cleared the air for all of us — for Gysbert van Tonder included. As a result, Gysbert van Tonder could for one thing sit more comfortably in his chair, relaxing as he sat. There was no longer any necessity for him to adopt a carefree pose which must have put quite a lot of strain on his neck and leg muscles, not even to talk of how hard it must have been for his spine to keep up that effortful bearing that was intended to suggest indifference.

Anyway, Gysbert van Tonder joined in the laughter that greeted Chris Welman's words. Constable Bothma laughed, also. It was clear from that that about the first thing the sergeant at the Bekkersdal headquarters must have told young Bothma was about how he had to keep an eye on Gysbert van Tonder.

It was good to feel that there was so much tension lifted from us then, after Chris Welman had spoken, and we had all laughed, and we understood that we need not pretend to each other any more.

"Of course, we know you haven't come here to spy on us," Jurie Steyn said to Constable Bothma, after a pause. "I mean, you've told us all that yourself. The little odds and ends of things that you put in your notebook — well, it's your job, isn't it? If you didn't write those little things in your notebook you'd get the sack, as likely as not. And if you didn't come and patrol my voorkamer, too, like you're doing now, you'd as likely as not also get the sack. And if you wrote anything in your notebook that isn't so, why, for that, of course, you would just get the sack, too."

From the way Jurie Steyn spoke, it would appear that, looked at from any angle, whatever Constable Bothma did, the one thing staring him in the face was dismissal from the police force.

"And there aren't so many things a policeman — I mean, an ex-policeman — can find to do when once he's got the sack," Jurie Steyn continued. "Because when you go and look for a job, afterwards, almost the first thing the boss will ask you is why you got the sack from the police. And no matter what your answer is, it always seems as though there is more behind it than what you say. Seeing that you are an ex-policeman applying for work the boss can never be sure about how much of what you are telling him is lies."

Johnny Coen took a hand in the conversation, then, and he said to the policeman that seeing that he and the policeman were both young, he could feel for the policeman. And he didn't want Constable Bothma to misunderstand what Jurie Steyn had just been saying, Johnny Coen went on. It was known that Jurie Steyn was like that, Johnny Coen said, but everybody knew that Jurie Steyn meant nothing by it.

It was just that we were all respectable people, respectable farmers, and so on, Johnny Coen explained, and for that reason we all got a little upset when a policeman came round, especially when the policeman pulled out a pencil and notebook. If we weren't such respectable people, respectable farmers and so on, Johnny Coen said, we wouldn't mind if even a dozen mounted policemen in uniforms came marching into our voorkamers with S.A.P. on their shoulders and with their horses waiting outside.

But it was just because we were respectable people that we got a guilty sort of a conscience when a policeman came into our house, Johnny Coen proceeded. And for that reason he wanted Constable Bothma to bear with Jurie Steyn and not to get offended at anything that Jurie Steyn said in haste.

"Oh, no," Constable Bothma said. "That is quite in order. I would not even have thought that there was anything insulting in it, in what Meneer Steyn said."

So Johnny Coen said that that was just what he meant. Any man that was not a policeman would very likely have had his pride hurt, by the way that Jurie Steyn had spoken. But he could see that it would, of course, be different with a policeman, Johnny Coen said. It wasn't that he thought a policeman didn't have *pride*—"

Johnny Coen looked pretty foolish, then. For he had been trying to stand up for Constable Bothma, but had only succeeded in making Jurie Steyn's disparaging references to the police force sound a lot worse.

After that it was, of course, Oupa Bekker's turn to talk. And although Oupa Bekker's story related to some period in the past when the functions of a police constable were exercised apparently not unsuccessfully by the local veldkornet, it seemed as though the difficulties that Constable Bothma was experiencing at present had some features in common with the vicissitudes that the young veldkornet in Oupa Bekker's story went through.

"Many a man would have been satisfied with that position," Oupa Bekker was saying, "just because of the honour that went with it in those days. For one thing, even if you didn't have a uniform or an office with a telephone in it to work in, like you have today, or even a mounted policeman horse with a white star on his forehead that can keep time to the music at the Johannesburg Show — even if you had to ride just one of your own horses on a patched saddle, and you had a patch in the seat of your trousers, too, you still had a printed certificate signed by the President to say you were veldkornet, and that you could hang in a gold frame on the wall of your voorkamer."

But the glitter of rank and the nimbus of office were as nought to that young veldkornet, Oupa Bekker said. The thing that worried the young veldkornet was that, because he was charged with the maintenance of law and order in his area, he was called upon, in however delicate a manner, to act as an informer on his neighbour. The thought that, through his job, he was cut off from intimate contact with his fellow-men saddened him. He liked having friends, and he found he couldn't have any, any more — not real friends — now that he was veldkornet.

"In the end—" Oupa Bekker said.

But we had rather that Oupa Bekker had not continued to the end, which was at once stark and inexorable, pitiless and yet compelling. For the only true friend that the young veldkornet had in the end was Sass Koggel, a scoundrel the like of whom the Groot Marico district had had but few in its history. Only with Sass Koggel did the veldkornet find, in the end, that he could be as he really was.

Sass Koggel and the veldkornet took each other for what they were. Neither, in his relations with the other, had to put up any sort of pretence. They were on opposite sides of the law. The veldkornet was all out to lay Sass Koggel by the heels. Sass Koggel directed all his efforts to the end that the veldkornet should get nothing on him.

But, outside of that technicality, it would be hard to find, in the whole of the Marico, a couple of firmer friends than were those two.

It was a long story that Oupa Bekker told, and we listened to it with fluctuating degrees of attention.

But Constable Bothma and Gysbert van Tonder did not listen to Oupa Bekker at all. They were too engrossed in what each had to say to the other. And while talking to Gysbert van Tonder, the cattle-smuggler, it was only once necessary for the policeman, Constable Bothma, to open his notebook.

Constable Bothma opened his notebook at the back, somewhere, and extracted a photograph which he passed over to Gysbert van Tonder. Gysbert studied the likeness for some moments. "Takes after you, does he?" Gysbert van Tonder asked.

In his voice there was only sincerity.

EASY CIRCUMSTANCES

"POVERTY is no crime," Chris Welman declared. He declared it loudly, a shade aggressively, at the same time pushing the toe of his broken veldskoen under his chair. "Nor is it a matter for shame, either," he added, "to be poor."

"No, I don't care who knows that I am not particularly rich, myself," At Naudé remarked, withdrawing from general view a trouser turn-up that had been mended with string. "Of course, it's not like I've been brought up poor. When my father trekked into these parts, coming up from the Cape, he was well-to-do. I won't say diamonds, and a sitting-up chair with blue curtains that you got carried around in, and such like, as they used to have in the old days in the Cape. No doubt my grandfather, in his time, would have been carried around in a sitting-up chair.

"But my father, when he came up from the Cape — why, we were just people in quite easy circumstances, that's all. Perhaps in the Transvaal — with the class of farmer living in the Transvaal then, I mean — we would have been thought to have been rich, even."

So Chris Welman said, yes, in the same way when his grandfather came up from the Cape his grandfather was reckoned to be a man of no little affluence — especially so, perhaps, in comparison with what was the financial standing of the general run of Transvaaler then resident in the Transvaal. In fact, he wouldn't have been surprised if his grandfather had actually been carried up from the Cape into the Transvaal bushveld, sitting in one of those sitting-up chairs with blue curtains.

"Yes, I can quite believe it," Gysbert van Tonder interjected in a sarcastic voice. "And it's easy to see that that's what your Nagmaal suit is patched with, too — with still a piece of that same blue curtain . . . Well, I'm not exactly penniless today, and I don't care who knows it. Also, I was brought up poor, and I'm not ashamed of that either."

So Jurie Steyn said, well, there were different ways of making money. And he wasn't sure that it would meet with everybody's approval, the way some people made their money. At the same time, he couldn't but think that it was a strange thing how some people would talk about their forebears that trekked up into the Transvaal from the Cape, and about how well-to-do their forebears were, compared with the Transvaalers there that lived just in reed and mud-daub houses.

After all, where did the Transvaalers that lived just in reed and mud-daub houses come from, if they didn't come from the Cape? He was sure he didn't know, Jurie Steyn said.

But what he would not seek to deny about his own family when they came up from the Cape, Jurie Steyn said, was that they enjoyed a greater than ordinary measure of prosperity. Compared with most of the Transvaalers, that was.

"Not that I won't admit that I'm myself a bit on the poor side, today," Jurie Steyn added, before Gysbert van Tonder could make another interjection. "And it's not that I'm ashamed of being poor, either. There's nothing about it that I've got to try and hide."

That was true enough. Shielded as his apparel was by the post-office counter, there were no flaws in his garments that Jurie Steyn needed to retire from the gaze of vulgar curiosity.

"It seems to me, though," At Naudé said, "that why the people living in this part of the Transvaal in the old days — living in their hartbees houses and all, in the bushveld — why they were, generally speaking" — he paused a moment to find the right word — "*flat*, was that they just perhaps didn't care so much in those days for riches. They were content to be poor. They knew there were more important things in life than just money."

Then Jurie Steyn said that, well, it was the same with us today, of course. We knew there were higher things than having the manager at the bank in Bekkersdal bowing and scraping to us, as though we were sheep farmers. And let a sheep farmer come and try to run sheep here among the thorn bushes of the Dwars-berge, where it was just made for blue tongue, and then see how it would be with that sheep farmer after a couple of seasons.

It just made him laugh, Jurie Steyn said, to think of that sheep farmer going to see the bank manager at Bekkersdal after that, and the sheep farmer getting treated by the bank manager like any one of us got treated. When Jurie Steyn made that last remark Chris Welman gave a short, harsh laugh. It was clear that Chris Welman was recalling some interview of his own with the Bekkersdal bank manager.

Thereupon At Naudé said that, speaking for himself, personally, he was glad to think that he, personally, had got inside himself a good deal of that fine spirit that the old Transvaalers already had inside themselves, in their wattle-and-daub and reed-and-daub houses, long before his own immediate forebears had even thought of trekking up from the Cape. He was glad to think that he himself today had higher beliefs than just to imagine that to be rich was everything. What was more, from what he had heard over the wireless, there was no guarantee that wool prices would always remain up there in the sky, somewhere, anyway.

Chris Welman laughed again. This time it was a more human, open-hearted sort of laugh.

"After all, where does it all lead to?" At Naudé continued. "All the money these sheep farmers are making, I mean. Those new lavish homes they're building with inside bathrooms that have got pipes going off right underneath the dining-room floor. And the walls painted smooth with cream paint like a looking-glass. Is that so much better than to have just a (his eyes swept along the walls of Jurie Steyn's voorkamer) "— just a ceiling of plastered-over Spanish reeds, with pieces of the mud coming away in places? Or uneven walls with huge brown splotches where the whitewash is peeling off in places? Or the clay marks there where the white ants went all that way up — at a time when Jurie Steyn's wife didn't have any paraffin or Cooper's dip in the house, I suppose?"

Jurie Steyn coughed uneasily. Maybe he was protected, all right, as far as his clothing below the level of the post office counter was concerned. But there was the whole of his voorkamer exposed in the nakedness of a poverty that — as we had all said in a manly way — we were none of us ashamed of. Jurie Steyn could not go and hide the walls of his voorkamer behind the counter, or thrust them out of sight under a riempies-bank, the while he declared that honest poverty was no sin, and that his people trekking up from the Cape had not been unacquainted with some of the hedonistic titillations imparted by creature comfort.

"The absolute filth, even," Chris Welman proceeded from where At Naudé left off, "of living in a pigsty like this — well, we all know it's just because that sort of thing doesn't worry Jurie Steyn, at all. He's above it. What I mean is, stink, even — "

That was when Jurie Steyn indicated to Chris Welman, in somewhat strong terms, that he reckoned he had gone far enough. Not that he didn't realise, of course, Jurie Steyn said, that both Chris Welman and At Naudé, in the remarks they had made, were only seeking to compliment him on the higher kind of attitude that he had to life, which led him to scorn low gain.

But there were limits to the amount of flattery a man could put up with, Jurie Steyn said. And, in any case, Chris Welman needn't talk. Just look about how careful you had to be where you put your feet down on Chris Welman's front stoep. Half the time you didn't know if it was a front stoep or a fowl hok, Jurie Steyn said.

Before the discussion grew really acrimonious, however, Oupa Bekker had begun to relate an old Transvaal story that introduced a good many of the features we had already touched on. It was a story of a poor girl, Miemie de Jager, who lived with her parents in the Groot Marico in the kind of hartbees house that we had already been talking about.

"It was the kind of dwelling Oupa Bekker started.

"You don't need to say that part of it again. We already know all that," Jurie Steyn interjected. For Jurie Steyn had noticed that At Naudé was again surveying his voorkamer in a thoughtful manner.

"Very well, I'll just say then that Miemie de Jager's parents didn't stay in exactly a palace—" Oupa Bekker proceeded.

"Yes," At Naudé nodded. "I can imagine just the kind of hovel she stayed in. I must say I think I've got a pretty good idea, now. And I think the less said about it, the better."

Thereupon Jurie Steyn burst out that At Naudé should be the last person to talk. If Miemie de Jager had ever seen At Naudé's kitchen, and the kind of plates he ate out of, Jurie Steyn said, then Miemie de Jager would feel, next to it, that her parents were rich people from the Cape who had just trekked in, sitting in sitting-up chairs.

Jurie Steyn talked as though he already knew what Miemie de Jager was like.

Only after Gysbert van Tonder had spoken at some length, and in a sneering way — saying that for people who weren't ashamed to be poor it was surprising how fussy some of us were — was Oupa Bekker able to get on with his story.

"Miemie de Jager," Oupa Bekker said, "lived with her parents in a — in just a plain house, that's all, that was near the first saw-mill that they had in this part of the Transvaal. And one morning, when she was on her way home again from the sawmill—"

"Good Lord!" Chris Welman ejaculated suddenly. "You don't mean to say they were that poor. You don't mean she worked in the sawmill — those heavy thirty-foot logs — that's no work for a young girl with fair hair and dimples — sawing—"

It was apparent that Chris Welman had already formed a picture in his own mind of how Miemie de Jager looked.

But Oupa Bekker said, no, it was just Miemie de Jager's father that worked in the sawmill. Miemie went there every morning to fetch fire-wood in a sack.

"And then that morning, on her way home through the blue-gums," Oupa Bekker continued, "she saw a young man approach along the path — a young man that she didn't know. She guessed right away that he must be a son of those new people that had bought up the sawmill and the whole property. Rich people from the Cape, they were.

"And so she let the sack of fire-wood fall from her shoulders quickly, and she hid the sack behind a blue-gum. She didn't mind the young man seeing her walking bare-footed, but she didn't want him to see her carrying that sack of wood. It went against her womanly pride. Not that she was ashamed of her parents being poor—"

No, no, we said. Poverty wasn't a crime, we said. But we had noticed Chris Welman hiding his broken veldskoen. And we had seen what At Naudé had done, furtively, almost, with his trouser turn-up, a little earlier on. So we knew just how Miemie de Jager felt about that sack, that symbolised how her parents were none too well off.

"She decided to walk straight on, and pass the young man, and then after he was out of sight she would go back and fetch the sack," Oupa Bekker said. "But after she had passed the young man — keeping her eyes down on the ground as she passed him — and she turned round to see if he was out of sight yet, she saw that he had turned round, to look back at her. And when he saw her turning round, he thought — oh well, they were both young. And so they walked slowly towards each other, Miemie de Jager walking much more slowly than the young man, and blushing a good deal.

"And the young man said that he was going to look at the sawmill that his father had just bought. And Miemie said that she had come out for a walk through the bluegums and to pick yellow veld-flowers. And they stood talking a long while in the pathway. And afterwards the girl said she had to go home, now. And then the young man said, oh, but what about her fire-wood. And he asked could he carry it home for her. And she said, yes. And when she saw him lift the sack of fire-wood on to his broad young shoulders, she knew that she would never need to carry a sack of fire-wood home again."

But Jurie Steyn wanted to know how Oupa Bekker knew all that. All about what went on in Miemie de Jager's thoughts, Jurie Steyn said.

"She told me after we were married," Oupa Bekker answered. "You see, I was that young man. It was my father that had just bought that sawmill. You must understand that, when we came up from the Cape to the Transvaal, my parents were in easy circumstances."

BEKKERSDAL CENTENARY

WE were talking about the centenary celebrations at Bekkersdal. They were doing it in real style, we said, and it gave us a deep sense of pride, in this part of the Marico, to think that our town, that we had regarded as just *being* there, kind of, should have so impressive and stirring a history, and what was more, a future resplendent with opportunity and promise.

"Well, I had never thought of Bekkersdal in quite that way before," Chris Welman said, "but when I went in week before last to have this tooth pulled out" — he inserted a couple of toil-discoloured fingers in his mouth to disclose the cavity — "I did notice a few of these centenary things they were talking about."

Chris Welman made some further remarks, but there was a certain lack of precision in his articulation through his holding his mouth open that way while he was talking.

After Jurie Steyn had said that with Chris Welman having his mouth so wide it was like there was a draught in his post office that he hadn't noticed before, and after young Vermaak, the schoolmaster, had explained about how he had been trembling, all the time, in fear that one of Chris Welman's fingers might slip into a part of his mouth where the teeth were still all in, and so get bitten off — in his classical studies at University he had read about a boxer who, having stopped one from a Greek boxing-glove, was spitting out teeth, the schoolmaster said, and he did not feel happy at the thought of somebody spitting out fingers on the floor of Jurie Steyn's voorkamer — after all that, Chris Welman said that he had a good mind not to go on talking any more about his impressions of the Bekkersdal 100th year celebrations, seeing how unappreciative we were.

And as for the Greek boxing-gloves that the schoolmaster had mentioned as what he had learnt about in the classics, Chris Welman said, well, they didn't seem, by the sound of it, to be much different from the brass boxing- gloves that members of the Jeppe gang just wore over the knuckles of the right hand.

And he did not think that the Jeppe gang were students of the classics so that you would notice it, much, Chris Welman said.

Thereupon At Naudé remarked that Chris Welman having a tooth out in Bekkersdal wasn't really of historical importance. It wasn't of much significance one way or the other, he reckoned. Especially today, with the newspapers and the wireless having a lot to say about Bekkersdal's centenary.

"If it had been a Voortrekker leader that had a tooth pulled out there a hundred years ago, it would have been different, perhaps," At Naudé continued. "If it had been the Voortrekker leader Andries Loggenberg, say, and it had been the time of the trouble between the Hervormde church and the Doppers, say — well, that would have been something.

"With Andries Loggenberg having his face all bandaged up, I mean, through the way they had of pulling out a back tooth a hundred years ago, well, he just wouldn't have been able to get on to an ox-wagon, then, and make a two-hour speech straight out of the Bible about what a blot on this part of the Dwarsberge the Cape Groote Kerk was.

"All he would be able to do, with his face all swathed in cloth like that, just his eyes and a piece of beard sticking out, would be to join a little in the hymn-singing afterwards perhaps, singing a few of the easier bass notes, that would still sound all right coming from behind the folds of dressing."

All the same, At Naudé informed us, we would be surprised to know what progress had been made in Bekkersdal in recent years. We would not perhaps observe it so much ourselves, he said, just going there to buy things, or to take produce to the market or to drop in for a talk with the bank manager to find out could we draw a little against next year's substantial cheques from the creamery that we were sure to get.

Indeed, it was actually in the course of a friendly exchange of views in that manner with the bank manager — the inkpot as likely as not upsetting on his desk from the way you were banging it to show him how amicable you felt towards him — that you might be inclined to feel that Bekkersdal had a considerable amount of leeway to make up, At Naudé said.

A ten-minute conversation with the bank manager could, At Naudé proceeded, leave you quite flabbergasted at the thought that Bekkersdal was only a hundred years old. The cobwebbed absence of forward-thinking, At Naudé said, the inability to keep pace with modern development that you encountered in that office with the leather-upholstered easy chairs that the doorman conducted you into when you had an up-to-date idea for the bank to be able to benefit itself by, was really astounding, seeing that the bank had to pay out nothing more than, immediately, a few hundred pounds in cash.

"'You've got *Founded in 1875* on the front of the bank,' Mr Coetsee,' I said to the bank manager last time," At Naudé informed us, "and I said to him, 'I see the *one* is so worn, you can hardly read it any more, through the years of wind and rain. And I think, well, you should just let it weather like that, Mr Coetsee. Because, from the ideas going on in here, it wouldn't be far wrong for this bank to have in front *Founded in 875.*'"

We felt that At Naudé was using rather a lot of words to tell us that he didn't get an overdraft. Well, we had more than one of us had that same difficulty. But we weren't so expansive about it. We merely said, in a few well-chosen words — short words — just what we thought of Mr Coetsee. And we said it, always, when Mr Coetsee wasn't there.

"But in other ways," At Naudé went on, when he saw that he wasn't getting any sympathy from us, "the town of Bekkersdal is advancing with rapid strides. There has been a lot over the wireless and in the newspapers about it. The newspapers have had mostly photographs and the wireless has had mostly what the Town Clerk says. Take population now.

"Well, I read the increase in population in the newspapers and

I heard it over the wireless. Did you know that there has been an increase in the white population of Bekkersdal during the last ten years of over 18 per cent? No, I didn't, either, but there has. And there has also been an increase in the Native population. But the biggest increase of all — and the Town Clerk talking over the wireless coughed a bit uncomfortably when he said it — was in the Indian population.

"And then, what do you think is Bekkersdal's income? No, I don't know the exact figures, either. But it's big, I tell you. It's big, not only for a municipality the size of Bekkersdal, but it's big also for a municipality a lot bigger. That's how everything that's going on in Bekkersdal is, it's big."

Because At Naudé was not able to quote exact figures, Chris Welman could revert to his eye-witness account of his recent visit to Bekkersdal that happened to coincide with some of the less exuberant features of the town's preparations for its centenary festival.

"I couldn't enjoy anything very much, of course," Chris Welman said, "on account of my tooth. I mean, even after it was pulled; it was just as sore, almost, as if it was still in. Except that, when it was still in, I didn't have to look every 20 yards or so for a likely place, not exactly in the street and not exactly on the sidewalk either, where I could spit — seeing that my tooth went on bleeding all day.

"Well, anyway, that was one thing I found out about a town, then. How hard it is, in a town, to find a place to spit. I mean, when you're on a farm, and you've got a few thousand morgen, none of it under irrigation, you can then just spit anywhere. And it needn't be because you've had a tooth out, either. Or because of the plug of chewing tobacco that you've got in your mouth. Or because of something you've just thought of.

"The thing is that on a farm you can just spit anywhere, and for no reason, and without thinking about it again. If you're taking a walk along the edge of your mealie-land, for instance, and there's been no rain, and you see what's coming up, on your mealie-land,

and more particularly what isn't coming up — and you happen to remember that you sowed there — why, there's no place at all, then, on the edge of your mealie-land, that you aren't allowed to come to a stop and stand and spit. And you can't do that just anywhere you like to in a town.

"But what I did come across quite a lot of in Bekkersdal was how enthusiastic everybody was about the progress the place was making. Like one man said to me how his daughter had been picked to dance in the Volkspele part of the hundred-year birthday celebrations of Bekkersdal. 'I don't mean she's dancing, actually,' he said to me. 'My wife and I would never allow that, of course. All my daughter does is she moves in Voortrekker costume in time to the Boere-orkes music — and you simply can't keep your feet still, when it's Boere-orkes music — and she is partnered by a young man also in Voortrekker costume, and she springs, too, naturally, when it comes to that portion of the Boere-orkes music, and the young man in Voortrekker costume springs, too, when it comes there, because he would look silly if he didn't just then, spring, but of course, I would never allow my daughter to dance'. They're holding the Volkspele on that piece of vacant ground where the next jam factory is going to be. How's that for progress, hey?"

Except for the schoolmaster, who said that it sounded a bit sticky — the jam factory part of it, he meant — we agreed that Bekkersdal was indeed making an impressive-sounding advance.

"And that old building with the thick walls and the small window-panes and the gable," Chris Welman went on, "that we called the old drosdy, standing right there in the middle of the main street — it must have been one of the first buildings they put up in Bekkersdal: I mean, it was just about stinking with age, what with those cracked tambotie-wood ceiling beams and those ridiculous iron gates that they say came from . . . oh, I just can't remember now, but they were so heavy, you could hardly push them open — well, the old drosdy is gone, now.

"You've got no idea how different the main street looks. A

man with a camera who came to photograph the old drosdy cried when he saw that it wasn't there any more. But they told him that he didn't have to worry, because that was where the new bioscope was going up that would have electric signs at night that you could see as far as Sephton's Nek. And he could come and photograph the new bioscope in a few months' time, they said to the man with the camera who was looking around him in a lost way, crying."

Right in our own time, too, we said, and never mind about the centenary celebrations, there had been a lot of progress made in Bekkersdal. Look at the year they chopped down all those oak-trees, we said, that lined the road going to the north. At least five miles of old oak-trees they must have chopped down, we said. And, well, how was that for advance? Didn't that show that Bekkersdal was really getting somewhere? On the map, wasn't Bekkersdal getting somewhere, we asked.

When people hinted, sometimes, that we weren't keeping pace with the on-coming floodtide of civilisation here in the Marico, well, there were a few things we could draw their attention to, all right. We spoke at considerable length, then, and Chris Welman was able to acquaint us with some of the details, that he had heard in the town, of the size of the sideshows that were going to be erected by the merry-go-round people who had contracted to help with the centenary celebrations.

"Is there going to be a merry-go-round?" Oupa Bekker inquired, his eyes lighting up. "Why didn't you say so before? Bekkersdal was named after my grandfather. But I didn't even think of going to the hundred-year birthday. I never thought they would have a merry-go-round, too. They're doing it grand, hey? The first merry-go-round I saw was when I was a child, and we had to go all the way to Zeerust. But you say they're really going to bring the merry- go-round to Bekkersdal? The horses going round, and brass music, and silver paper stars?"

"More than anything else, silver paper stars," Chris Welman said.

Oupa Bekker was genuinely excited.

"My! My!" he said, and again, "My! My! To think that after all these years such a thing should happen to Bekkersdal. We're all going, of course, aren't we? Bekkersdal's hundredth year's birthday. What Chris Welman says is as good as a centenary, just about. And brass music and silver paper stars."

We all said yes, of course we would go. The only person that seemed a bit out of it was the schoolmaster.

And because what he said was what he had learnt at University, the schoolmaster's words did not make sense to us, overmuch.

"The drosdy," young Vermaak said, "gone. It's like the front teeth knocked out of Bekkersdal's main street. It's as though I've had my own front teeth knocked out by a caestus. It's like I'm myself spitting out teeth."

"Silver paper stars," Oupa Bekker said, who hadn't heard what the schoolmaster was saying, and wasn't interested, anyway.

SIXES AND SEVENS

"SMELLS good," Gysbert van Tonder observed. His manner was expectant.

"Tastes good, too," Jurie Steyn replied, with his mouth full.

Jurie Steyn was seated behind the counter. In front of him was a dish of mieliepap and ribbok ribs that he was eating mainly with his fingers.

"Cooked it myself, too, with the wife away in Johannesburg," Jurie Steyn continued, in between taking a kick at a couple of mongrel dogs that were fighting under the counter over a bone that he had thrown on the floor.

"Sets you up, a good feed like this does," Jurie Steyn added. "I cooked it just on the ashes of a fire I made next to an anthill. No nonsense with a kitchen stove. I don't understand a kitchen stove."

In the main, we agreed with Jurie Steyn that we did not have much understanding of the workings of a kitchen stove, either. We would have agreed with him on anything, then.

A few minutes later Chris Welman came in.

"Smells good," Chris Welman remarked. His voice sounded hopeful.

"Cooked it myself," Jurie Steyn answered. "Just on the ashes."

Not long afterwards At Naudé came in at the front door.

"Smells good," At Naudé said, coughing in an insinuating way.

"Just on the ashes," Jurie Steyn informed him.

It was only natural, then, that we should spend some time in discussing sundry aspects of the culinary art as practised in the open. Cooking on a fire made next to an anthill, we said. Or made next to a boulder. Or made just next to nothing at all. And then you didn't need such a thing as a pot, either, we said, except maybe for the mieliepap. And for that just a tin would do, also.

And you needed hardly such a thing as a kettle, either, except, of course, for the coffee. And cooking out in the open we didn't need plates, at all. In fact, about all you ever used a plate for, out in the veld, was to dish the food into, that you'd cooked. And we didn't need such a thing as a knife and a fork and a spoon, either, we said, except maybe just to eat with.

About then, Oupa Bekker arrived. "Smells—" Oupa Bekker began. "— on the ashes," Jurie Steyn declared.

From there Gysbert van Tonder started to talk about how much simpler life was on a farm than in a city; and about how much more enjoyable it was, too. You never felt that you were really alive in a city — not really living, that was. Take Johannesburg, now, Gysbert van Tonder said. It was all just big shops with plate-glass windows and bright lights and bioscopes and saloon bars with green curtains in front of them. Could you really call that living, spending your days in a place like that, Gysbert van Tonder demanded.

And so Chris Welman said, no, it was too awful to think of it, even. Especially the saloon bars with the green curtains in front of them were too awful to bear thinking of, Chris Welman added, reflectively passing the back of his hand over his mouth as he spoke.

"And you don't really need cups, either," Gysbert van Tonder remarked, reverting to his consideration of the simple delights afforded by the great outdoors, "except maybe just for drinking coffee out of."

"Or a razor, either," young Vermaak, the schoolmaster, supplemented, "except perhaps just to shave with. In fact, it seems to me that you don't need anything out on the veld, except just to use that thing for what it was meant for."

Naturally, young Vermaak would talk like that, we felt. Since he was a schoolmaster, it was only to be expected that he would miss some of those finer points, which you had to be born and bred on the veld to be able to understand.

"Actually, what I feel for city people," Chris Welman said, "is just pity. I mean, just think how miserable a person from the city looks, when he comes to a farm, to visit. Right here in the Marico, even, I've seen it."

"It's particularly when the farmer shows the visitor from the city over his lands," Gysbert van Tonder interjected. "And the farmer explains to the visitor where he's going to plough, next year, and where he's going to sow sugar beans. And the farmer takes the visitor right round the twenty-morgen patch where the barbed-wire fence is to come for the new camp, but where there is now just nothing but thorn bush."

Yes, Chris Welman agreed, and at the end of it, through his having accompanied the farmer through that stretch of thorn bush, it would appear to the visitor from the city as though the barbed wire that the farmer had been talking about was already there, in place. What would give the visitor from the city that illusion, Chris Welman said, was the way his sports blazer looked, consequent on the visitor having been through those thorns.

"What makes it even more miserable," Jurie Steyn declared, pushing aside his empty plate with a gesture expressive of contented repletion, "is when the visitor acts as though he enjoys it all. You get that sort, too. Queer idea of enjoyment, though, I must say. Give me just a plain piece of ribbok — just roasted on the ashes. That's all I ask."

Thereupon Oupa Bekker said that, speaking for himself, he wouldn't ask much more than just about that, either. With, say, perhaps just a slice of raw onion to go with it. It was funny, though, that when Jurie Steyn was out there by the fire, it didn't occur to him that he would that afternoon be having visitors in his voorkamer. Seeing that Jurie Steyn's was the only farm in those parts where you could still get an occasional ribbok in the rante, Oupa Bekker said, expressing what we all felt, there would have been no harm in his having roasted a few more pieces.

"I did," Jurie Steyn said, "roast a few more pieces. And I ate them."

Even though we had really come there just for our letters and milk-cans, At Naudé remarked, we were still, in a sense, visiting Jurie Steyn. And if he had been properly brought up, Jurie Steyn would have treated us accordingly.

Jurie Steyn puffed at his pipe with an air of deep satisfaction.

"I know you're a visitor," Jurie Steyn said to At Naudé, "but with my wife away, I can't be as polite as I would like to be. I've got nobody to look after this place. But if you'll wear your Nagmaal jacket next time you come, I'll be glad to show you all over my farm where I'm not going to plant potatoes next season. That is, among the haak-en-steek thorns."

It was clear that this was not one of Jurie Steyn's friendly days. Perhaps all that ribbok he had eaten was already beginning to disagree with him.

"All the same," Chris Welman said, after a pause, "I can't see that there's anything so very much wrong in having a bit of fun at the expense of somebody that comes from the city to visit you on the farm. I don't mean anything rough, like playing tricks on a person, for instance, because he's a stranger."

So we said, no, that positively was something we could not associate ourselves with, either.

"What I mean is all right, for instance," Chris Welman continued, "is to push a small likkewaan down the back of a visitor's neck, and to pretend to him that it's a mamba. Now, there's no harm in a little joke like that, and it's usually also very amusing for the children. And what there's nothing wrong with, either, is when you're with a visitor in the bush at night and you tell him that almost anything that he sees stirring is a mamba. That's also just fun. And so is also, when he's in bed, pulling a length of hosepipe over the visitor with a piece of string, and making out to him that that's a mamba. You see what I mean? I don't believe in playing pranks on a stranger."

In his list of playful deceptions which could, with advantage, be practised on visitors from the city, Chris Welman did not betray any marked originality. Nor did he make it clear as to the stage at which a jest ceased being broadly funny and became a prank. Maybe it was the stage at which a mamba actually bit a visitor. Maybe it was that sort of thing, too, that imparted to a visitor from the city that aspect of a peculiar melancholy of which we had already made mention.

"After all, we haven't got very much that we can entertain ourselves with, here on the veld," Gysbert van Tonder agreed with Chris Welman. "And it gets so lonely here, too, sometimes, with only the bush and the koppies, that you can go just about mad, almost."

"Whereas, in a city, people have got everything," Chris Welman said. "If you want something from a shop you haven't got to drive eleven miles there. And there are bioscopes. And all the people on the sidewalks. And the bright lights at night. And there is also — "

"Yes," Gysbert van Tonder said, "with a green curtain in front."

"Taking a visitor from the city over your farm," Jurie Steyn said, musingly. "Well, my grandfather was great on that. Right until the time of his death, my grandfather would tell this story, and laugh. What made it even funnier, as far as my grandfather was concerned, was that this visitor from the city, who wore a black frock-coat, actually was entitled to be shown all over the farm. For the visitor had come from the city with a lot of papers to buy my grandfather's farm. And my grandfather sold the farm to the visitor, my grandfather getting fifty pounds more for the farm than what he had paid for it. But, all the same, my grandfather just couldn't resist having a joke with the visitor. And because there wasn't any bush on the farm, seeing that it was a highveld farm, my grandfather got the visitor in his long frock-coat and all to climb through a barbed wire fence, instead, quite a number of times. And why my grandfather laughed so much was because the visitor didn't know it was the same barbed-wire fence that he was climbing through, each time."

Jurie Steyn paused to pull at his pipe some more. And in between he informed us that he had also been having a little joke on us, that afternoon, seeing that we were visitors.

"I've got a piece of ribbok meat wrapped up for each of you in the kitchen," he said. "I'll fetch it out for you when the lorry comes. But if you'll take my advice, you'll get your wives to cook it for you properly on the stove. It's no good roasted on the ashes. For one thing, all the gravy runs to waste. And it also tastes queer, cooked just on the ashes. I don't know where the old people got that idea from."

After that he started talking about his grandfather again.

"Whenever my grandfather told this story," Jurie Steyn said, "he would laugh so much that he would slap the top part of his leg, laughing. But there was one side of the story of the farm that my grandfather sold for fifty pounds more than he paid for it that my grandfather never used to lay stress on, that you would notice. And I only understood that side of it properly when I went on a journey one day to the highveld to go and have a look at that old farm again. And I had great difficulty in finding it, seeing that everything about it had changed so much. They had even changed the name of the old farm. They now called it Benoni. And there was a mine head-gear where the stable had been.

"And I have often thought since then of how that visitor from the city must have laughed when he told his side of the story — how he must have slapped the top part of his leg, I mean, laughing.

"And it doesn't seem to me as though it's shreds of the stranger's frock-coat hanging on the barbed-wire fence. It's like it's my grandfather's own clothes hanging there, blowing in the wind."

ILL-INFORMED CRITICISM

IT was some visitor from foreign parts who, just before leaving, made certain remarks to newspaper reporters about what he thought the Transvaal platteland was like. At Naudé retailed some of those remarks to us. "Primitive" was one of the words that visitor had used about us, At Naudé said. And "mediaeval", the visitor had remarked. And he also had said "work-shy".

Listening to all that from At Naudé in Jurie Steyn's voorkamer, that afternoon, we were, naturally enough, pained.

"Mediaeval!" Oupa Bekker snorted. "Well, I don't know what that word means, not having heard it more than twice or so before in my whole life, unless it was said, maybe, by somebody talking fast, so that I couldn't *catch* it. No, I don't know what that word means. But taken along with those other things that get said about us, from time to time, I should imagine that mediaeval is just about the worst of the lot."

Oupa Bekker said the word over to himself several times. Mediaeval. You could see there was something in the sound of it that, in spite of himself, Oupa Bekker liked.

"Now, just imagine a man like that visitor," Oupa Bekker continued. "He couldn't even have seen the country, properly—"

"He said he had seen enough," At Naudé interjected.

"And then he says these things about us," Oupa Bekker went on, "and then he gets out — quick. He's away in an aeroplane before anybody can prove to him that we're not mediaeval. That's one way, now, where I don't hold with progress.

"For instance, in the old days, if a visitor, passing through Derdepoort, say, made a remark like that about the platteland, why, we would have caught up with him before he had got to the Malopo. And we would have proved to him, right there by the camel-thorns, with a sjambok, how mistaken he was in saying that we were savage and unpolished and — and backward — and things like that. I can't call them all to mind, right now."

Gysbert van Tonder suggested a few words to help Oupa Bekker out. And then we all remembered one or two extra words that had also been said about us at various times. It was with a sense of pride, almost, at the end, that we realised how many words there were, like that, that had been said about us, by visitors from foreign parts.

But it was evident that Oupa Bekker's thoughts were still on that traveller who was now thousands of miles away, riding in an aeroplane through the sky.

"Even if they had just the train to Ottoshoop, still," Oupa Bekker declared, sounding wistful, "we would yet have been able to point out to that visitor where he went wrong. We would have been able to point it out to him with a short handkarwats on the station platform."

Anyway, what At Naudé had repeated to us from the newspaper report did awaken our interest. Chris Welman turned to the young schoolmaster.

"What does it mean, now, Meneer Vermaak, mediaeval?" Chris Welman asked. "I suppose that visitor means we're just a lot of stinking —s, his saying we're mediaeval? Or a lot of pot-bellied —s, hey, with our feet sticking out sideways like a muscovy duck's? Is mediaeval as low a word as all that?"

Thereupon Jurie Steyn said that Chris Welman had no occasion to use such expressions, especially as his wife was in the kitchen, and might hear. Moreover, Chris Welman could speak for himself. Chris Welman could be as mediaeval as he liked, Jurie Steyn said. He didn't care. But he himself didn't wish to be included in being called a stinking —, thanks. He wondered where Chris Welman learnt such awful language.

"It's all right, Jurie, your wife isn't in the kitchen," Chris Welman was able to explain. "She's on the roof. I saw her when I came along. Just listen, you can hear her hammering there, now. When I came along she was sawing."

"Must be trying to fix that chimney, I suppose," Jurie Steyn observed. "It's been all over to one side since that big wind we had."

We all sat well forward and Oupa Bekker put a hand up to his ear when the schoolmaster, having cleared his throat, explained that mediaeval had to do in the first place with the feudal system. Chris Welman looked startled. He thought he knew all the low words there were, Chris Welman said. And what he didn't know himself he had learnt the time, long ago, when he had been a white labourer in Johannesburg digging foundations. But the word feudal was a new one on him. He hoped the schoolmaster wouldn't let it slip out by accident in the schoolroom one day, in front of the children, when he lost his temper about something, Chris Welman said.

But the schoolmaster went on to explain further. And it was a long sort of explanation. And it didn't seem to lead anywhere. It seemed like it had to do with history, and in the end we were several of us yawning. There was no point to it.

From what the schoolmaster was saying, Oupa Bekker commented, it would appear that the word "feudal" had to do with some kind of government. And so he didn't see where the schoolmaster's explanations fitted in, at all. For that matter, he didn't expect that that kind of government was much of an improvement on what we had right here in the Groot Marico.

"Most of those things you're talking about we've already got," Oupa Bekker said. "So what's the argument?"

"It seems to me that it's some more of that progress talk," Gysbert van Tonder announced. "Well, we don't want any more of their progress, mediaeval or any other kind. They can go and have all the progress they want somewhere else, if they like. But they can't come and have it on my front stoep, they feudal well can't. And as for that visitor saying we're work-shy — well, does he know what work is, at all, I wonder? Him sitting in that aeroplane, all snooty."

For a good while after that we each of us started wondering the same thing, each of us wondering, in turn, if the visitor had ever pumped water for the cattle in the hot sun. Or if the visitor had ever chased a pig to put in a crate, in the hot sun, for several hours, with the visitor's family and the Mtosa farm-hands falling over each other, all the time, and the boss-boy going to the police afterwards — the boss-boy claiming that the visitor had kicked him on the ear on purpose when the pig jumped out of the crate again.

Or if the visitor had ever got a letter from the store keeper at Ramoutsa about what he would do unless the visitor made a big payment in three days, in the hot sun.

We all spoke about some time or other that we had worked.

The longest story of all was Chris Welman's. He had to take so long over it, not because he was working so much, but because it was the time he was in Johannesburg, digging foundations, and he had to tell us a lot of things about what Johannesburg was like, in those old days. There was a lot of labour trouble at that time on the Rand, Chris Welman said. And almost every other day they were having a general strike. He wasn't quite sure what it was all about, Chris said, but he wouldn't say it didn't suit him. It just meant that every so often he would have to put down his spade and pick and go home.

And they had a woman Labour leader that they called Miss Florence Desborough, Chris Welman said. He had never seen her, but he would have liked to, he said.

Not that she would ever have taken any notice of his sort, he knew. But he pictured what she was like from her name. And he thought of her as pretty, and having a soft, refined voice, and with an ostrich feather in her hat and having high-up shoulders, like they wore in those days. He got all that just out of the sound of her name, he said — Miss Florence Desborough.

And then one day there was again a general strike that he and his mates, standing digging in a trench, didn't know about. How they got informed, Chris Welman said, was when one of those old-fashioned taxis that they had in those days drove right up to where they were working, and a woman came dashing up to them out of the taxi, swinging a pick-handle, that was tied to her wrist with a piece of string. She was screaming, too, Chris Welman said. And he himself didn't stop running for about six blocks. Anyway, he himself was a bit disappointed, afterwards, when he learnt that that woman had been Miss Florence Desborough, and that she had the nickname of Pick-Handle Flo.

Jurie Steyn's wife, coming in at that moment with our coffee, didn't sound very different from Miss Florence Desborough, we thought. Moreover, Jurie Steyn's wife had a black smudge on her forehead from the chimney.

"What do you call yourselves?" she asked indignantly. "Of all the lazy, good-for-nothing loafers — talk, talk, is all you do. Here I have had to get on to the roof myself with a hammer. And a saw. And a pick. Who's ever heard of a white woman having to swing a pick?"

Jurie Steyn's wife said a lot more. We did not answer her.

"One thing, at least," Oupa Bekker chuckled, after Jurie Steyn's wife had gone out again. "One thing at least that she didn't say is that we're mediaeval."

FAILING SIGHT

WE did not think that the picture in the newspaper that At Naudé passed round to us was particularly funny. After all, it wasn't the first time we had known of a Bapedi chief that had got over his troubles with a motor-car that way.

And, as Chris Welman pointed out, so many things had already been said about motor-cars, and about the things that happened to motor-cars, that that sort of picture didn't raise a laugh any more.

"Even at the Gaberones end of the Dwarsberge, where the sand starts," Chris Welman proceeded, a perceptible disdain in his voice at the thought of there actually being so unsophisticated a region, "even there they don't think it's funny, today, when a man takes a car to the garage and they find after two days that why it won't go is because it hasn't got petrol."

"Or through the engine having got stolen out of it by some mine-boys passing through there on their way back to Rhodesia," Gysbert van Tonder supplemented, "the garage taking two days to find out that the engine wasn't there at all."

Generally speaking, yes, we were inclined to agree with Chris Welman. Jokes about a motor-car were pretty stale. There didn't seem to be much point in At Naudé having gone to the trouble of cutting that photograph out of the newspaper and passing it round to us in Jurie Steyn's voorkamer. For we all knew that sort of thing. But At Naudé insisted that we had missed the true purpose of his having brought that newspaper cutting along. Had we studied the picture carefully, he asked.

"But that's what we've been saying," Jurie Steyn, whose turn it was with the photograph, observed. "We've known of a Bapedi chief doing exactly the same thing before. And it's not so very funny, I don't think. After a person had had a lot of trouble with a motor-car I can quite imagine that he would come to believe that that was the easiest way out — removing the engine, because it's just so much unnecessary weight, and inspanning a good team of long-horned oxen to pull the motor-car, instead. There's nothing unusual about it, any more. Another thing, I'll go so far as to say it's sensible."

While there might have been nothing very unusual about the photograph, it was certainly not customary for Jurie Steyn to acknowledge that a Bapedi chief could do anything sensible. It was the schoolmaster's turn to examine the clipping.

"It's not so much that it's an old joke, although it is that, too, of course," young Vermaak said, "but it's also an old photograph. Take that jacket, now, that that white man has got on sitting in the car next to the Bapedi chief. It's years since they stopped making jackets with that narrow kind of lapel. And look how straight up the white man is sitting. It looks as though he's very proud to be in a motorcar. Or to be having his photo taken. Or to be sitting next to a Bapedi chief.

"And the car — why, I've never seen so old-fashioned a model. And that headlight sticking out behind the ox's ear — it's the kind of lamp we used to light to go to the stable with when I was a boy. The only part of the picture that looks up-to-date is the trek-chain fastened on to the car's bumper. And as for the white man's moustache — well, there's an old model-T for you, if you like."

The schoolmaster said that, as far as he was concerned, it actually was a funny photograph. And it wasn't the circumstance of the motor-car being drawn by a span of oxen that made him laugh, either. The real scream was that moustache.

Studying the old photograph in his turn, Oupa Bekker said that maybe it was an old joke. But he had nothing against an old joke, himself. Indeed, some of the old jokes were the best, Oupa Bekker said. For one thing, they lasted longest.

"Only, Rabusang doesn't look like that, any more," Oupa Bekker added, shaking his head.

"But Rabusang never did look like that," At Naudé said, laughing. "It's not Rabusang but some other Bapedi chief. All it has got printed under the photograph is 'Bapedi chief cheerful about petrol shortage'. It doesn't say which Bapedi chief."

At Naudé went on to say that it was a bit of a showing-up for Oupa Bekker, his making a mistake like that. For it was well known that Oupa Bekker, while admitting that his hearing might not perhaps be what it once was, always claimed that his eyesight was as good as ever.

"But I've just said that he doesn't look like Rabusang," Oupa Bekker explained, getting petulant. "How do you expect me to say it any clearer than what I've just said it? I've just said that Rabusang doesn't look like that — not unless he's changed a good deal with the years. This Bapedi chief doesn't look like Rabusang any more than that white man there with the silly moustache looks like Rabusang. In any case, the light's not too good."

Oupa Bekker didn't say whether it was the light that he himself was sitting in at that moment, or the light in which the two occupants of the motor-car had sat years ago when the photograph was taken.

"In any case," Oupa Bekker proceeded, quickly, apparently anxious that his failing powers of vision should not be made the subject of a lengthy and detailed disquisition, "I also once travelled quite a distance in a motor-car that a Bapedi chief had taken the engine out of and that was being pulled by a long span of oxen.

"It was before daybreak. I was going by ox-wagon to Ramoutsa. We had started early and there was that thick mist that hangs over the turf-lands by the Malopo on winter mornings. The voorloper was carrying a lantern to see the road. I was walking by the side of the wagon. And it was in the light of the lantern that we saw a motor-car on the road in front of us.

"A motor-car was a new thing in those days, and so I guessed that it must be the motor-car that Chief Umsufu had bought some time ago. I was surprised that it was going so slowly, though — not even at walking pace. It must be that some part of the machinery wasn't working like it should, I thought. Or perhaps Chief Umsufu had put the brakes on, I thought, since he might prefer not to go so fast in the dark.

"Afterwards, the driver put his head out of the window. Out of curiosity to see how a motor-car went, I had by that time got almost level with the motor-car, so that Chief Umsufu and I both recognised each other by the light of the voorloper's lantern coming on behind.

"When Chief Umsufu told me I could have a lift I climbed in pretty quickly. It was the first time I had ever been in a motor-car and I didn't want to miss any of the ride. It was only afterwards, when it got properly daylight, that I could see through the mist what it was that was making the motor-car move, and I felt pretty disappointed, then, I can tell you. But I didn't get out then, all the same. For one thing, it wouldn't be polite, I thought.

"And then, for another thing, it was, after all, a motorcar that I was riding in, and for years to come I would be able to talk about it, telling people about how I once went to Ramoutsa in a motor-car. And there would be no need for me to say that it was Chief Umsufu's motor-car and that it was being pulled by a team of oxen. What I might mention, perhaps, was that the motor-car was not travelling particularly fast, that time, because of the roads.

"But, in the meantime, sitting in the motor-car on that early morning and not knowing that the engine part of it was rusting by an anthill next to the chiefs cattle-kraal, I must say that I got a lot of enjoyment out of the journey.

"I could feel by the soft cushions that it was a very good class of motor-car. And then, also, the motor-car didn't make a noise I already knew that you could tell it was a good motor-car if the engine was silent. And I don't think there has ever been a motor-car engine as silent as Chief Umsufu's was, on that misty morning. In fact, in talking to the chief, I hardly had to raise my voice at all, to make myself heard.

"Another thing I noticed was that there seemed to be lots of cattle on the road. I saw, a good number of times, through the mist when it lifted slightly at intervals, a pair of horns or the back part of an ox. At times I also heard what I took to be cattle-drovers shouting out Sechuana words. Some time later I began to realise that it was the same words, all the time. And when day broke I saw clearly that it was also the same pairs of horns."

Gysbert van Tonder said, in a nasty way, that it would appear that already in those days Oupa Bekker's faculties had started failing.

"Either that, or—" Gysbert van Tonder said, concluding the remark with a gesture to indicate that, as likely as not, Oupa had been drinking.

"What Chief Umsufu said to me afterwards," Oupa Bekker continued, "was that it was because he believed in progress that he had bought the motor-car in the first place. But I would never believe what trouble he had with it, the chief said. And then he found out that what was wrong with an ordinary motor-car was that it didn't have enough progress.

"And so he used his brains and worked out how to remedy it. And since then he had had no trouble at all with his motor-car, he said. And he didn't have to worry any more about what the roads were like, either. Where an ox could go, there his motor-car could go, too, now, the chief said. And also where a mule could go. You could see that he was very proud of what he had done. 'Engelsman!' the chief shouted at the oxen, 'Witvoet! Lekkerland!' at the same time bringing his foot down on some piece of machinery that, I suppose, would have made the motor-car go faster in the days when the engine was still there, before Chief Umsufu used his brains on it."

Thereupon Chris Welman said that, as he had mentioned earlier, there was nothing funny any more in stories that had to do with motor-cars. The long story Oupa Bekker had just told proved that, Chris Welman said. Since the motor-car had come into the Transvaal, life on the platteland was no longer the same thing.

The only kind of story about the Transvaal that was worth listening to, Chris Welman said, was a story about the Transvaal before there were motor-cars, or before they had that machine on Rysmierbult station that you put pennies in for chocolates.

"Or before they had cameras," At Naudé said. Then he asked Oupa Bekker if there was already a photographer at Ramoutsa, the time he went there with Chief Umsufu's motor-car. Oupa Bekker, after reflecting for a few moments, said, yes, he thought there was.

"And did you have your photograph taken?" At Naudé asked. "Before the motor-car was outspanned, even?"

After thinking about it for a bit, Oupa Bekker said, yes, he did seem to remember something about it.

"Well, take another look at that, then," At Naudé said, passing the newspaper cutting back to Oupa Bekker. "I said that nobody had studied it properly. Who do you see sitting in that motor-car? Don't laugh too loudly, now."

Oupa Bekker examined the bit of newspaper carefully.

"Yes," he said, at length. "Yes, it does look something like Chief Umsufu. In fact, it is Chief Umsufu. I would recognise him from this photo anywhere. But when I said at the start that it wasn't Rabusang—"

"Nobody is talking about Rabusang," At Naudé interjected, sounding cross. "But who's that white man, sitting there large as life, next to the chief? Don't laugh, now."

Oupa Bekker looked at the picture some more. Then he handed it back to At Naudé.

"It's no good," Oupa Bekker said. "It's some white man I don't know. Some white man with a silly-looking moustache. But, of course, that sort of moustache was worn quite a lot, in those days."

DYING RACE

IT was these scientists, Jurie Steyn said, coming along into the Kalahari and studying the Bushmen and their ways and listening to what they had to say, that were giving the Bushmen wrong ideas. How a self-respecting white man, and one supposed to have a certain amount of education, too, could waste his time like that passed his understanding, Jurie Steyn said.

And he wasn't talking even about how much of the Bushman's time got wasted. For the Bushman needed every spare moment of time he had, Jurie Steyn reckoned, in order to be able to meditate properly on what kind of a lost heathen he was.

"That's the only way the Bushman will ever get right," Jurie Steyn said, "through sitting down and using his brains a bit — thinking out quietly about why he's such a bane to mankind. It's only in that way that he'll be able to change his ways a little and not get the human race such a bad name wherever he goes just through his belonging to the human race."

But instead of that, there were these scientists actually coming along and studying the Bushman's ways, and making notes, Jurie Steyn said. What could the Bushman think other than that his manner of life was all right, and something to be proud of, even, when white men came and asked him questions about it, telling him that they were anxious to learn about his habits?

That gave the Bushman no end of a high opinion of himself — thinking that white travellers had come all that way into the desert just to look him up so that they could learn from him. It made the Bushman quite insufferable, Jurie Steyn contended. The Bushman stuck his chest out, and acted as though he was some sort of a professor, talking just any kind of rubbish that came into his head as though it was the most profound wisdom.

"I've known," young Vermaak, the schoolmaster said, winking, "more than one University professor that was just like that."

"You'd think that a Bushman would be only too glad to keep quiet about his habits, seeing what most of his habits were," Jurie Steyn continued. And he wasn't talking even about a Bushman's habits to do with laundry that he saw hanging on a clothes-line when there was nobody within sight. Or a Bushman's habits with a sheep that had strayed from the flock and the shepherd having his back turned for a few minutes. Or his habits with watermelons that you weren't watching. Or with a blancmange pudding when the pantry window was open.

There was the Bushman's established practice, Jurie Steyn said, of going down on all fours in front of an anthill that he had broken the top of off, and just licking up the ants as fast as he could go, and without washing them first. And his custom of popping a scorpion in his mouth and swallowing it down without chewing, not even thinking under what kind of a stone that scorpion might have been. And then patting his stomach afterwards.

Naturally, it gave a Bushman wrong ideas about things, Jurie Steyn said, when a well-dressed white man, instead of asking him wasn't he ashamed of himself for being so low, said that he had come to the Bushman to learn, and started making gramophone records of the things the Bushman had to say. Or a film.

"I even heard one of those records," Jurie Steyn added, "and you know what, I could hardly understand what the Bushman was saying, with all the extra clicks he put in, him thinking he's so smart, talking into a gramophone. But what I say is, if a scientist wants to study something, why can't he go and learn something high up? Like high dictation — or — or —"

"Or ethnology?" the schoolmaster suggested. "Or anthropology?"

"Yes, something high up like that," Jurie Steyn agreed. "What's he want to fool around with studying Bushmen? The scientist can take it from me that no good can come of that. Next thing, he'll also be patting his stomach after eating something that he didn't take the insides out of first."

Another thing, At Naudé said, that was causing a quite unnecessary amount of disorder in these parts, was that story that the scientists had been spreading of late about the Bushmen being a dying race. Every year their numbers were decreasing, the scientists said. Soon the Bushmen would be no more.

Gysbert van Tonder said he was glad At Naudé had mentioned that, because he was coming to it.

"As though the Bushmen haven't always been cheeky enough," Gysbert van Tonder said. "And now here's this new piece of nonsense, about the Bushman disappearing. Well, we all know, of course, that when it's with something slung over his shoulder that doesn't belong to him, then there's nobody can disappear as quick as a Bushman. I mean, when you look again, he's just vanished. And, of course, that's what happens every time with the scientist. The scientist is sitting out in the desert on a camp-stool with the recording instrument on one side of him and a bottle on the other, and the Bushman is talking.

"And when the scientist hears the machine going click-click-click quicker than what the Bushman is making clicks, he knows it's time to change the record. And, naturally, when the scientist turns round again, the Bushman isn't there any more. And because he's absent-minded, being a scientist, he doesn't see that the bottle isn't there any more, either. And because he doesn't notice the Bushman around, he thinks, ah, well, the Bushman must be dead. It's only a scientist that would get hold of a muddle-headed notion like that, of course. Or what do you think?"

We did not demur.

"And the advantage," Gysbert van Tender proceeded, "that the Bushman is taking of this tomfool story that he is dying out, is just too awful. He thinks he's something precious, because he's dying. Like I said to a Bushman in the Kalahari a little while ago, no, he couldn't have any more chewing tobacco. He'd had enough for one morning, I said . . . So what does this Bushman answer? 'You'll be sorry for this one day, baas,' he says. 'One day when I am not here any more. When all that will be left of me will be a gramophone record.' "

When he did feel sick, though — really sick — Gysbert van Tonder said, was when the Bushman said it would be a happy release for him.

"I got him in the end, though," Gysbert van Tonder remarked, looking pleased with himself. "He was loafing on the job. So I told him to shake himself. 'Hurry up,' I said to him, 'you know you haven't got too much time.' "

We said to Gysbert van Tonder that it was easy to see that that one couldn't have been a very raw Bushman. The only part of him that might have been raw, we said, would be the inside of his hands — raw from trying to make a fire by rubbing two sticks together in front of a movie camera.

There was another side to being a film actor that was different from just getting your name in front of a bioscope in electric lights, we said. And the Bushman was beginning to find that out for himself. For one thing, he also had to start thinking out silly answers to the questions the scientist asked him. Because, unless he gave a silly answer, the scientist would think he wasn't a proper Bushman, and that would be the end of the Bushman's film and gramophone career.

"It makes you sick," Gysbert van Tonder — who was apparently not feeling quite himself that afternoon — said for the second time. "Like one Bushman that a scientist asked 'What happens when you throw a stone into the water at Lake Ngami?' . . . and the Bushman said, 'It makes brass bangles come on the water, baas.' Now, that Bushman just about choked, trying not to laugh. He knew as good as you or me that if you chuck a stone into a dam it gives off yellow ripples, with the sun shining on them.

"But the Bushman knew that, to have a film made of him as the last survivor of a primitive race, his answer had to be as absurd as possible. And you've got no idea what a fuss the scientist made of that Bushman, who was trying not to choke. The scientist said to the camera-man that they must have a close-up of the Bushman right away."

He felt like choking himself, too, Gysbert van Tonder said. With indignation.

"It made my stomach turn," he pursued in the vein of earlier on. "And so I said to them, well, if that Bushman is now becoming a film star, the next thing he'll want is to be allowed to wear a collar and tie, and to vote. And then the scientist said that he was sorry he was a bit short of film, because he would like a close-up of me, also."

But just to think, Gysbert van Tonder observed finally, that the Bushman had today already grown so ignorant that he couldn't make a fire any more by rubbing two sticks together, but had to use matches. It might even be true, Gysbert van Tonder suggested, what the scientists said about the Bushman — that he was a member of a dying race.

But young Vermaak, the schoolmaster, advised us not to be too hasty in our conclusions. All the scientist was doing, he said, was to try and trace back the story of man to its beginnings. How man rose from savagery. How he started inquiring after truth. How he attempted decoration early on in his upward march. How he followed his destiny, with science and knowledge as his guides. Maybe the Bushman was the wrong person for the scientist to come and ask these questions of, the schoolmaster said, but it was a fact that, belonging to a very primitive division of African humanity, the Bushman was a true prehistoric type. And maybe the first cave-man would also have liked to play-act before a movie camera, pretending he didn't know more than a stone-axe.

"And what we've been saying about the Bushman's ignorance," the schoolmaster added, half laughing, "well, we know he's a member of a dying race. Face to face with the King of Terrors. You know what I mean — The Great Adventure, and all that. Anyway, it's queer to think that — with all his ignorance — the Bushman will *shortly know more than any of us.*"

NEIGHBOURLY

A fence between the Union and the Bechuanaland Protectorate, At Naudé said. According to the radio, the two Governments were already discussing it.

"I hope they put gates in the fence, though, here and there," Chris Welman said, "otherwise how can we get to Ramoutsa siding?"

Yes, with a fence there, At Naudé agreed, goods we had ordered from Johannesburg could lie for years at the siding, and we none the wiser. "And likely as not we wouldn't even notice the difference," At Naudé added. "We'd think it was just the railways again a bit slow."

There was one queer thing about putting up a fence, Oupa Bekker said, that he himself had noticed long ago. And it was this. When you erected a fence around your farm, it never seemed to keep anybody out. All you were doing was to fence yourself in, and with barbed wire.

In the meantime, Gysbert van Tonder, with his somewhat extensive cattle-smuggling interests, had been doing a spot of thinking. When he spoke, it was apparent that he had been indulging in no glad, carefree reveries. His reasoning had followed a severely practical line — as straight as the five-strand course, theodolite-charted, of the fence that would provide the Union and the Bechuanaland Protectorate with official frontiers.

"There should be a proper sort of a border: that I do believe in," Gysbert van Tonder announced piously. "It makes it a lot too hard, smuggling cattle from the Protectorate into the Transvaal, when there's no real line to smuggle them over. I'm glad the Government's doing something about it. These things have got to be correct. I've got discouraged more than once, I can tell you, asking myself well, what's the good. You see what I mean?

"Either you're in the Marico, or you aren't. And either you're in the Protectorate or you aren't. When there's no proper border you can be standing with a herd of cattle right on the Johannesburg market and not be feeling too sure are you in the Transvaal or in Bechuanaland. Even when the auctioneer starts calling for bids, you don't quite know is the answer going to come in pound notes or in rolls of brass wire.

"You almost expect somebody to shout out 'So many strings of beads'. So I can only say that the sooner they put up a decent kind of fence the better. The way things are, it's been going on too long. You've got to know if an ox is properly smuggled over or if it isn't. You've got to be legal."

The years he had put in at cattle-smuggling had imparted to Gysbert van Tender's mind an unmistakably juridical slant. He liked arranging things by rule and canon, by precept and code. The next question he asked bore that out.

"In this discussion that our government is having with the Protectorate government," he asked, "did the broadcast say rightly what kind of fence it is that they are going to put up? Is it the steel posts with anchoring wires kind that you cut? Or will it have standards that you pull out and bend the fence down by the droppers for the cattle to walk over on bucksails? That's a thing they should get straight before anything else, I'm thinking."

The conversation at that point took, naturally enough, a technical turn. The talk had to do with strands and surveyors, and wrongly-positioned beacons and surveyors and rails, and the wire snapping and cutting Koos Nienaber's chin open in rebounding, and gauges and five-barb wires, and the language Koos Nienaber used afterwards, speaking with difficulty because of all that sticking plaster on his chin.

"And so the surveyor said to me," Chris Welman was declaring about half an hour later, "that if I didn't believe him about that spruit not coming on my side of the farm, then I could check through his figures myself. There were only eight pages of figures, he said, and those very small figures on some of the pages that didn't look too clear he would go over in ink for me, he said.

"And he would also lend me a book that was just all figures that would explain to me what the figures he had written down meant. And when I said that since my grandfather's time that spruit had been used on our farm and that we used to get water there, the surveyor just smiled like he was superior to my grandfather. And he said he couldn't understand it. On the other side of the bult, in a straight line, that spruit was a long way outside of our farm.

"What that other surveyor, many years ago, was up to, he just couldn't make out, he said. With all his books of figures, he said, he just couldn't figure that one. Well, I naturally couldn't go and tell him, of course. Although its something that we all know in the family.

"Because my grandfather had the same kind of trouble, in his time, with a surveyor more years ago than I can remember. And when my grandfather said to the surveyor, 'How do you know that the line you marked out on the other side of the bult is in a straight line from here? Can you see through a bult — a bult about fifty paces high and half a mile over it?' — then the surveyor had to admit, of course, that no man could see through a bult. And the land surveyor felt very ashamed of himself, then, for being so ignorant. And he changed the plan just like my grandfather asked him to do.

"And the funny part of it is that my grandfather had no knowledge of figures. Indeed, I don't think my grandfather could even read figures. All my grandfather had, while he was talking to the land surveyor, was a shotgun, one barrel smooth and the other choke. And the barrels were sawn off quite short. And they say that when he went away from our farm — my grandfather having proved to him just where he went wrong in his figures — he was the politest surveyor that had ever come to this part of the Dwarsberge."

There would, he said, then, unquestionably be a good deal of that same sort of element in the erection of the boundary-wire between the Bechuanaland Protectorate and the Transvaal. More than one land-surveyor would as likely as not raise his eyebrows, we said.

Or he would take a silk handkerchief out of his pocket and start dusting his theodolite, saying to himself that he shouldn't in the first place have entrusted so delicate an instrument to a raw Mchopi porter smelling of kafir-beer.

In the delimiting of the Transvaal-Bechuanaland Protectorate border we could see quite a lot of trouble sticking out for a number of people.

"I also hope," Jurie Steyn said, winking, "that when the Government sends up the poles and barbed wire for the fence to the Ramoutsa siding, there isn't going to be the usual kind of misunderstanding that happens in these parts as to whom the fencing materials are for. I mean, you'll have farmers suddenly very busy putting up new cattle camps, and the fence construction workers will be sitting in little groups in the veld playing draughts, seeing they've got no barbed wire and standards."

Anyway, so there was a fence going to come there, now, along the edge of the Marico, through the bush. Barbed wire. A metal thread strung along the border. Sprouting at intervals, as befitted a bushveld tendril, thorns.

"A fence now," Chris Welman said. "Whenever I think of a fence, I also call to mind a kindly neighbour standing on the other side of it, shaking his head and smiling in a brotherly-love sort of way at what he sees going on, on my side of the fence. And all the time I am just about boiling at the advice he's giving me on how to do it better.

"Like when I was building my new house, once, that was to provide shelter for my wife and children. And a neighbour came and stood on the other side of the fence, shaking his head at the sun-dried bricks in a kind-hearted manner. Turf-clay was no good for sun-dried bricks, he told me, seeing that the walls of that kind of stable would collapse with the first rains. And I didn't have the strength of mind to tell him the truth. I mean, I was too ashamed to let him know that I had really meant those bricks for my house.

"So I just built another stable, instead, which I didn't need. And it was only a long time afterwards — through a good piece of the mud that he had smeared it up with in front crumbling away — that I found out that my neighbour's own house, which he always talked in such fashionable language about, was built of nothing more than turf clay bricks, sun-dried."

Yes, Jurie Steyn said, or when you were putting up a prieel for a grapevine to trail over.

"And then that neighbour comes along and says, what, a shaky prieel like that — it'll never hold up a grapevine," Jurie Steyn continued. "And then you say, well, it's not meant for grapes, see? You're not that kind of a fool, you say. You're only making a trellis for the wife. She wants to grow a creeper with that feathery kind of leaves on it, you say.

"And then your neighbour says, well, he hopes it isn't very heavy feathers, because it won't take much weight on it to bring that whole thing down. By that time you feel about like a brown weevil crawling over one of the sideshoots of the grapevine you intended to plant there. And it's a funny thing, but you never really take to the blue flowers of the creeper that you put in there, instead."

It was significant, we said, how you would on occasion come across a stable that looked far too good for just an ordinary bushveld farm, with squares and triangles in plaster cut out above the door of the stable. And with a stoep that, if you didn't know it was a stable, why, you could almost picture people sitting drinking coffee on it. And spidery threads of creepers twining delicately if somewhat incongruously about solid scaffoldings with tarred uprights. Looking as though why the farmer made the pergola so sturdy was that the pale gossamer blooms shouldn't just float away. And it would all be because of the advice of a neighbour who had at one time stood on the other side of the fence, kind-hearted, but with his eyes narrowed.

Almost as though he couldn't believe what he was seeing there. And his one hand would be resting easily on the wire, as if at any instant he could jump clean over and come and take what you're busy with right away from you, and show you how it should be done. His other hand would be up to his forehead so that he could see better. And he would be shaking his head in a kindly fashion in between making recommendations.

That was what a fence represented to us, we said. Young Vermaak, the schoolmaster, made a remark, then. It was the first chance that he had had, so far, to talk.

As far as he could see, the schoolmaster said, the effect it was going to have — erecting a fence between the Union and the Bechuanaland Protectorate — was that it was going to make the Union and the Protectorate really neighbourly.

THE RECLUSE

IT was significant that when we spoke of him it was as Meneer Lemare or as Old Lemare. It wasn't merely that we didn't know his first name, but that, moreover, we didn't want to know it. And on those rare occasions when he emerged from his cottage in the leegte that was all grown about with the thorniest kind of cactus, his encounters with Marico farmers were not characterised by any noteworthy degree of cordiality.

It was like talking to a more disappointed kind of one of his own prickly pears.

"I remember, years ago, when I came across him on the road to Ramoutsa, and I told him my name was Naudé, and I asked him how he was," At Naudé said. "He told me to voetsek."

Then Jurie Steyn mentioned the time, long before he had his post office, even, when he came across Old Lemare in the Indian store. And Old Lemare was telling the Indian to voetsek, Jurie Steyn said.

"I thought of telling Lemare that it wasn't right that a man should live all by himself, the way he was doing," Jurie Steyn proceeded. "There was something from the Good Book that I wanted to mention to him in that connection. It was from Deuteronomy IX of the Good Book. But I decided afterwards rather not to say anything to Lemare about it."

"Was he carrying that thick stick with a piece of brass fastened on the end of it?" At Naudé asked.

Yes, Jurie Steyn acknowledged, that did have something to do with his changing his mind about talking to Old Lemare about the disadvantages of a life in solitude. "And although I didn't say anything to him," Jurie Steyn added, "when I was going out of the store, he called out to me, all the same, to voetsek."

That was what happened, of course, the schoolmaster said,

when one retired from society, carrying under one's arm a pick-handle loaded with brass. One's vocabulary grew limited. A few simple words sufficed for the elementary day-to-day needs of the hermitage.

"But it needn't be as simple as just to say voetsek," At Naudé remarked gruffly. "A hermit doesn't need to be as day-to-day as all that."

Johnny Coen said that it sounded as though Old Lemare must have suffered some great disillusionment, in the past. Something must have blighted his hopes. The cup dashed from his lips, and so forth. And that was what had made him like that.

"Yes, you can see he's frustrated," the schoolmaster said. "It's a rather heavy stick, too, I should imagine? And the brass work on it pretty solid?"

Jurie Steyn nodded.

"I thought so," the schoolmaster said. "He's probably an infantile romanticist and he's not making a constructive utilisation of his vital energies and reserves. And so what would do him good would be a straight talking — to in plain words—"

"Words like voetsek," At Naudé interjected, readily. "You go and talk to him like that. We'll wait for you outside. Outside that clump of prickly pears."

The schoolmaster ignored At Naudé's pleasantry and went on to talk of the mature individual's need to meet reality objectively in every situation and of about how creative self-realisation would make Old Lemare throw away that stick, this leading to an increase in his conversational powers.

What the schoolmaster said did not make much sense, and Chris Welman — who had so far not been taking much part in our talk — several times tried to interrupt the schoolmaster with something he himself wanted to say.

"Maybe Old Lemare got that way long ago through some love affair," Johnny Coen said, eventually. "Maybe some heartless girl with a pretty face and yellow hair jilted him. There is that sort.

122

And perhaps she had long lashes, too, that curve up at the ends."

"But I tell you, it's like this —" Chris Welman started again. Only, he didn't get any further, because Gysbert van Tonder began talking then.

And Gysbert van Tonder said that if there was a girl in it, as far as Old Lemare was concerned, then the shoe might just as well have been on the other foot. It might have been that it was Old Lemare that had jilted that girl with the fair hair and the eyelashes for a newer sweetheart, and that when he was out driving in a spider all polished up with his new fancy, what should happen but that the girl he had forsaken should appear by the side of the road and, being lovelorn, should start throwing mule-dung at them, so that his new girl's satin dress and picture hat would be all ruined and so she wouldn't speak to Lemare again, blaming him for it — women being known to be unreasonable in that way.

While we agreed that a tendency towards anchoritism in the individual would possibly be given stimulus by the circumstances Gysbert van Tonder had conjured up, we had no reason for supposing that that was what had happened in Old Lemare's case — especially as there was so little we knew about him, actually.

This time Chris Welman had his say.

"Lemare's name is David Goliath Ebenhaeser Philip Lemare," Chris Welman said. "He was born at Groot Drakenstein in the Cape on January 18.. . . . I forget the year, now, but I can look it up. He is a European (White) and he has an income of £15 a month from two houses, brick, that he owns in Fordsburg. He is the head of his house, here, and Piet Sikazi (Bechuana) stands in relation of servant to him. Piet gets a wage of £1 3s. 6d. a month and an egg with his mieliepap every Wednesday. Lemare has got seven fowls that are not inoculated against Newcastle sickness, and a pig that is. He must have read the instructions on the bottle wrong. He's also—"

"All right, Chris," Gysbert van Tonder said, "we all know you were a census enumerator. And if you think it's funny to go and tell everybody what people fill in on their census forms, then

I must say that I can't see the joke in it. And I'm not thinking of myself either. I'm not ashamed of the whole world knowing everything that's filled in on my census form. But I'm thinking of other people, that aren't as fortunate as I am myself in this way, perhaps. I am as much as anything else thinking of my neighbours, who might have things they wouldn't like known."

Jurie Steyn said then, too, in a pious tone, that he was also just thinking of the other man when he spoke about how low it was for an enumerator to go around blabbing. We all of us made remarks in similar terms, some of us getting quite heated. It was good to discover the deep sense of loyalty that the Marico farmer entertained towards his neighbour. It was something that one would hardly have suspected, ordinarily.

"It makes your blood boil to think of your private affairs being bruited about all over the place," At Naudé said. Then he added quickly, "your neighbour's private affairs, that is."

Oupa Bekker had just begun talking about a vile census enumerator they had had in the old days — Blue Nose Theron, they called him, and also Blue Nose something else that Oupa Bekker would not like to repeat because he liked to keep the talk clean — when Johnny Coen noticed that Chris Welman was moving somewhat uncomfortably in his chair.

"It's all right, Chris," Johnny Coen said, "we're not blaming you for anything. We all know it must be a hard and thankless job, being an enumerator, and when At Naudé said just now that no decent man would take it on, he didn't mean you. He was thinking of that Blue Nose man, likely."

"But Oupa Bekker hadn't started talking about that Blue Nosed — yet, when At Naudé said that," Chris Welman replied, sounding aggrieved. At the same time, we couldn't help feeling that the epithet Chris Welman applied to Blue Nose was a lower word even than Oupa Bekker had been thinking of.

"Anyway, somebody else can have the job of enumerator next census," Chris Welman went on, "and when it comes to my form I'll put it in a closed envelope fastened down with sealing-wax, and then I'd like to see some Blue Nose — try and find out things about me, that's all. I say a man's private life isn't safe with these low snoopers."

Having relieved his feelings in that way seemed to put Chris Welman in a much better mood. And we were inquisitive, of course, about Old Lemare. Scandal-mongering and prying into other people's affairs were — as Jurie Steyn had pointed out — things that we left to census enumerators.

But we felt that it would be instructive for us to know a bit more about Old Lemare. Like what sort of bed did he sleep in, we would like to know. And we couldn't help thinking that his kitchen must be in too awful a state for words, with dirty plates and pots all over the floor. And we would like to know if the tenants in his Fordsburg houses paid their rent regularly. And we wondered if Old Lemare and the pig washed in the same dish.

We wouldn't have minded asking Chris Welman such questions. For the interest we took in Old Lemare was quite different from just prying.

"Yes," Chris Welman said, in reply to a question by Johnny Coen, "it was because of a woman that Old Lemare decided to withdraw from the world — armed. That stick weighs eighteen pounds, he says, with brass and all. Old Lemare used to be a lecturer, in the old days—"

Jurie Steyn whistled.

"Well, I hope he used more words in his lectures than what he uses today," Jurie Steyn said. "And I hope he also told his listeners more things than just telling them to get the hell out of it, like he does now."

But Chris Welman said that was just what Old Lemare had told people in his lectures — telling them that they would go to hell if they didn't lay off drink. Old Lemare was a temperance lecturer, Chris Welman said, and it seemed that temperance lectures were very popular in those days.

We all said that that was something we couldn't understand, quite. It looked as though Old Lemare was already a bit queer in the head even then, we said, thinking that people would come along and hear him talk about stopping drinking.

"He said it wasn't so much the men that came to listen to him as the women," Chris Welman explained, "and he said there was one woman, Sister Getruida, that used to go ahead and make arrangements at the places where he was going to talk, and he had an understanding with Sister Getruida, and he was hoping to marry her, some time, because he admired how good she was at organising committees and hiring halls.

"Then, one day, he came to Barberton to lecture and when Sister Getruida met him at the station she said that Barberton was a mining camp and a very sinful place, and Old Lemare noticed on her breath that she had been eating peppermints — because of her cough, she said.

"And then he found out that the hall wasn't booked, because of her cough, and then by the evening he noticed that the smell of peppermint on her breath was stronger than ever, and she turned her head sideways when she spoke to him, so that the smell of peppermint shouldn't upset him, she said.

"Well, it was very sad for Old Lemare when, next thing, Sister Getruida got a job as a barmaid, and because he couldn't get on without her, he used to go and sit in the bar drinking lemonade and Sister Getruida would laugh at him, and say he wasn't a man at all, all the while that one of the customers, a commercial traveller, called her his baby-faced angel."

Afterwards, when he came to the bar again, Chris Welman said, to look for the commercial traveller, with that brass-shod stick, Old Lemare found that Sister Getruida had run away with the commercial traveller — flown away, likely, seeing the name that the commercial traveller had given her. And that was the story about how Old Lemare had become a recluse.

There was an interval of silence after Chris Welman had finished talking.

"Is it — is it all true?" Jurie Steyn asked.

"True?" Chris Welman snorted. "It's as true as Oupa Bekker's lies about that Blue Nose Pete, whoever he is. Or as true as Gysbert van Tender's rubbish about the fair-haired girl throwing manure at the couple riding in the spider. It's as true as anything I've told you about Old Lemare. You don't think I'd really be so mad as to go to his house in the middle of the cactus with a census form, do you?

"No, I just filled in his census form the best way I could by guessing everything, including his Christian names and his servant Piet, and the two houses in Fordsburg.

"I just guessed all that. And if the authorities don't like it, well, I would like to see how much would be left of the authorities if they went round with a census form to Old Lemare."

MARICO MAN

WE were talking about the fossil remains discovered in a gulley of the Malopo by Dr Von Below, the noted palaeontologist. Dr Von Below claimed that what he had found were the remains of the First Man. And it was going to do us on this side of the Dwarsberge a lot of good, we said, especially as Dr Von Below had paid us the compliment of giving his discovery the name of the Marico Man.

The distinguished professor had already given a talk over the wireless about the Marico Man that At Naudé has listened in to. And the schoolmaster, young Vermaak, had read an article on the Marico Man in a scientific magazine to which he subscribed.

"The professor made his find using just the simplest tools you can think of," At Naudé informed us. "Just a simple digging-stick and a plain hand-axe."

"Sounds like the professor is a bit of a Stone Age relic himself," the schoolmaster observed, "using that kind of tools." Nobody laughed.

The important thing, the schoolmaster added, when his joke hadn't gone over, was that as a result of this discovery the Marico Man would now take his place alongside of the Piltdown Man and the Neanderthal Man all over the world in scientific circles where the question as to who was the First Man on earth was being discussed. It was an inspiring thought that the Groot Marico was the ancestral home of the human race.

"That here in the Dwarsberge the First Man, millions of years ago, lower than any savage, started painfully on his upward progress," the schoolmaster said.

But Jurie Steyn said that, speaking for himself, he wasn't too keen on that "lower than any savage" part. Especially as the professor had decided to call his discovery the Marico Man, Jurie

Steyn said, with a quick wink at Chris Welman that the school-master did not intercept.

"Yes, that's true," Chris Welman said, coughing and also shutting and opening his left eye too quick for the schoolmaster to see. "I must say I don't fancy it, either — calling an ignorant creature like that the Marico Man. It's that sort of thing that gives us Marico farmers a bad name."

And we didn't want any worse name than what we already had, Chris Welman reckoned.

"And look now what it says about the professor finding the Marico Man's remains in a ditch," Jurie Steyn continued, almost spluttering at the thought of the way that he and Chris Welman were pulling young Vermaak's leg. "Right away people will start getting to think we're so low here that when a person dies his relatives don't give him a proper Christian burial but they just go and throw him away in the fist ditch they see. Next thing they'll say is that the Marico Man was found buried with a clay-pot next to him. And beads."

By this time Gysbert van Tender had also tumbled to what was going on. If it was a bit of fun at the schoolmaster's expense, he didn't mind joining in himself.

Frowning on the suggestion of Bushman obsequies in relation to the Marico Man, Gysbert van Tender declared that he would "rather just lie in the veld and get eaten up by wild animals than to be buried with the Bushman religion. For one thing, what won't my children think of me, I mean, when we meet in the next world and it comes out that I was buried according to the Bushman religion? Or take the Pastor of the Apostolic Church, now, that I told to his face how un-Christian his Nagmaal service was that I looked in at through the window of his church and saw.

"I can just imagine how tight the Pastor will draw his mouth when he comes across me in the hereafter, me having been buried under a half-moon and with an ostrich egg painted blue. I'd feel that I was walking with nothing more than a stert-riem on, in the hereafter."

Not able to keep his face as straight as the Apostolic Church Pastor's, Gysbert van Tonder burst out laughing. And so he pretended that he was just laughing at the incongruity of the thought of himself wearing a Bushman's wildcat-skin loin-cloth. "Isn't that a scream," he asked, "the thought of me wearing a stert-riem in the hiernamaals?" When nobody answered, Gysbert van Tonder's face fell.

It seemed a bad afternoon for jokes. The only people who appeared to be enjoying themselves were Jurie Steyn and Chris Welman.

They kept it up quite a while, saying silly things about how much discredit the Marico Man was going to bring on the inhabitants of the Dwarsberge area, and doing their best to sound earnest.

"People all over the world will think we don't even know enough to have an ouderling saying words at the graveside," Jurie Steyn was announcing.

"But what's all this talk of funerals and the rest?" the schoolmaster interrupted, looking perplexed. "It's not as though the Marico Man died just the other day, after a long and painful illness that he bore with a patience that was an example to the whole of the Dwarsberge. He's got nothing to do with anybody living here now. So I can't understand your talking about him almost as though you're feeling sentimental about him. After all, it's millions of years ago since the Marico Man was on the earth."

It was when Jurie Steyn, choking over his words, started to say that that was what made it all the more sad, that young Vermaak realised what Jurie Steyn and Chris Welman had been up to.

The schoolmaster thought deeply for a few minutes.

"Anyway, it's like this," he said, eventually. "We know that it can do us a lot of good, in these parts, to have the Marico Man. He's going to make our district world-famous. In radio talks and newspapers, in lectures and theses and textbooks, wherever the Neanderthal Man and the Piltdown Man get mentioned, the Marico Man will have to be spoken of, also. Now, that's something, isn't it? Quite a bit of an achievement for a South African, don't you think?"

Young Vermaak recognised, however, that a certain element of jealousy crept into these things. Even the world of science was not altogether immune from that regrettable spirit of partisanship which, in the education department, for instance, could lead to a man who had only a Third Class Teacher's Certificate getting appointed to an A-post over the head of somebody who had excellent academic qualifications, failing only in blackboard-work.

"And I still say," young Vermaak declared — speaking, as it were, in parenthesis — "that, give me a piece of chalk that writes and a blackboard easel that doesn't fall over backwards the moment you touch it — the department examiner hopping about directly afterwards, holding his one foot — then I still say I'm as good at blackboard-work as the next man."

We felt that it would have been in better taste, on young Vermaak's part, if he had abstained from drawing aside the veil that had, until then, screened from public gaze the circumstances attendant on his having got low marks in one of the subjects he took for his teacher's diploma.

"I am only trying to explain," he continued — closing, in a somewhat self-conscious fashion, the parenthesis — "that in the scientific world there will as likely as not be prejudice against the Marico Man. And just because he's so good, that is, they'll have spite against him. And so they won't sometimes mention his name when they ought to — like when they're mentioning the Neanderthal Man's name, say, or the Piltdown Man's name.

"He's great, I'm telling you — the Marico Man is. As a claimant for being the First Man, why, the Marico Man has got the Piltdown Man licked hollow. And as for the Neanderthal Man — I really believe that next to the Marico Man the Neanderthal Man hasn't got a leg to stand on, leave alone two legs and two hands to stand on, which I believe is how the Marico Man actually stood, if the truth were only known. That is how good I think the Marico Man is.

131

"And so you can quite understand that there would be scientists that would be jealous of the Marico Man, and they would talk slightingly of him.

"They don't like to have to accept it that their Neanderthal Man went up like a rocket but came down like a stick, the moment the Marico Man arrived on the scene — arriving on the scene walking on all-fours, even, and with his mouth hanging sort of half-open in surprise.

"There are going to be scientists that will hesitate to let on, in fashionable places, that they have even heard of the Marico Man. And all just because they think he's a bit too crude. Everybody naturally expects the First Man to have been somewhat rough. But when he's just out-and-out offensive, like it looks as though the Marico Man must have been, well, you can understand that quite a lot of scientists are going to be pretty haughty in their treatment of him. Especially when they've got the future of their pet, the Neanderthal Man, to think of. Or their other pet, the Piltdown Man. His career. Next thing they know, the Piltdown Man will be out of a job. He'll be on the sidewalk, cadging sixpences for drink."

Needless to say, the way the schoolmaster put it then made it all look different. If there was going to be prejudice against the Marico Man, merely because he came from this side of the Dwarsberge, well, we wouldn't stand for it, that was all.

"I'd like to know what right they've got to despise the Marico Man," Jurie Steyn said, "just as long as he did the best he could, while he was alive. That's what I say. Just so's they can crack up one of those — what are they, again?"

"The Neanderthal Man?" the schoolmaster asked. "The Piltdown Man?"

"Yes," Jurie Steyn said, "those. A couple of foreigners — immigrants — that a Marico-born man has got to stand cheek from, when he's just as good."

The point, the schoolmaster said, about the Marico Man, was not only that he did his best, but that he achieved far more than any of his closest rivals in the competition for being acclaimed the First Man. From the shape of his skull, you could see that the Marico Man had all the opposition beaten to a frazzle in respect of weakness of brain-pan.

The Marico Man was so much slower-witted than the Piltdown Man that it was pitiful. Pitiful for the Piltdown Man's chances of getting recognised as having been the First Man, that was. Nobody, no matter how primitive, had any chance of being accorded senior classification as a human being, when all the time there was the Marico Man lurking in the background. *Skulking* in the background would probably be a more accurate way of expressing it.

It was a solemn thought, the schoolmaster said, to contemplate the Marico Man as we knew him — the Marico Man supporting himself in an upright position with the help of his knuckles, his eyebrows lifted high and his jaw protruding several inches more than the Neanderthal Man's jaw. The Marico Man in that particular posture, looking at a planet. It made you think, the schoolmaster said.

Gysbert van Tonder was the first to tumble to it that in all this long thing he was saying the schoolmaster was just being sarcastic — on account of his leg having been pulled earlier on.

"But I still say," Gysbert van Tonder declared, doggedly. "With all this nonsense that has been talked, I still say that if the Dr Von Below knows what is good for him, he'll keep away from this part of the Dwarsberge. We won't think twice of running him out of the place. Running him and his precious Marico Man out of the place. And seeing which of them goes quicker. What I can't get over is the cheek of this scientist — digging up a handful of bones and calling it the Marico Man. And talking about him walking almost four-footed; and having a weak brainpan; and a jaw like a gorilla; and—"

"It's a closely reasoned treatise," the schoolmaster said. "I've read it."

"About the only insulting thing," Gysbert van Tonder observed, "that this scientist doesn't say about the Marico Man is that the Marico Man is also cross-eyed and left-handed."

This was one of those days when Oupa Bekker was somewhat more deaf than usual. He had heard and followed only part of our conversation.

"The first man in the Marico?" Oupa Bekker asked. "You mean, the first Marico white man? Well, that's Louw Combrink . . . Louw Toutjies, we used to call him in the old days. He used to walk sort of bent forward . . . Hey? What's that? . . . No, not his beard. It's the way his jaw stuck out . . . Louw Toutjies? . . . Of course, he's still alive. He's living in the mountains just other side Derdepoort . . . Scientist? Well, I'd like to see what Louw Toutjies does to a scientist that's been telling people he's dead. I'd like to see it, that's all."

GLOSSARY

"Ander Man se Kind" — "Another Man's Child"

"Die Nooi van Potchefstroom" — The Girl from Potchefstroom, the title of a popular tune.

"En in my droom," — And in my dream

"Is die vaalhaarnooi by die wilgerboom" — the fair-haired girl is at the willow tree.

"Vertel my neef, vertel my oom, is dit die pad na Potchefstroom?" — Tell me, nephew, tell me uncle, is this the road to Potchefstroom?

Abba-kitchen — A back kitchen, the word "abba" being of Khoi origin as in carrying a child on one's back.

Arnosterbos — A heath like shrub found in the western parts of South Africa, often used as a herbal remedy for minor ailments.

Baas — Boss, master, particularly used by Africans to refer to whites.

Backveld — The back country, isolated countryside.

Bakhatla — A member of a tribe of the Tswana people, also the language they speak.

Baksteen — Brick.

Bapedi — Another word for the Sotho tribe.

Basie — Small boss, diminutive of Baas. Often used to refer to young whites.

Bechuana — An African tribe, today known as Tswanas.

Bechuanaland Protectorate — Today known as the country of Botswana, then a British colony.

Bioscope — Cinema.

Bitter-bessie — A small shrub whose berries have a bitter taste.

Boeremusiek — Boer music, popular light music, often for dancing, usually based on Afrikaans folk music and played by a small band which usually includes a concertina or piano accordion.

Boere-orkes — A band which includes a combination of concertina or piano accordion, mouth organ, fiddle or guitar, and percussion, and plays Afrikaans popular music.

Cape Zwartland — A region of the Western Cape, called the "black land" because of the tendency of the local bush to tale on a dark appearance after heavy rains.

Cape-cart — A two-wheeled hooded carriage, drawn by between two and eight horses,

Dominee — A parish clerk in the Dutch Reformed churches.

Doppers — A nickname for a member of the strictly Calvinist Reformed Church in South Africa.

Dorp — Town.

Drosdy — A magisterial and administrative office, now obsolete.

En — And

Engelsman — "Englishman", an English-speaking white South African.

Geoutoriseerde — Authorised,

Groot Marico — Greater Marico (Marico being the region where the stories are set).

Groote Kerk — Great Church, mother church of the Dutch Reformed Church in South Africa.

Haak-en-steek thorns — "Catch and stab" thorns, from a large, flat-topped deciduous thorn tree.

Handkarwats — A short-handled riding whip; a quirt.

Hartbees house — A house, hut, or temporary shelter of simple construction, usually consisting of an A-shaped thatched roof, sometimes with low reed walls.

Hervormdes — A name often given to members of the Nederlands Hervormde Kerk, or Dutch Reformed Church.

Hiernamaals — Afterlife.

Hok — An enclosure for domestic animals.

Kaboe — Boiled (formerly also roasted) whole maize kernels.

Kafir-beer — An alcoholic beverage made by made by malting, drying, grinding, boiling, and fermenting millet.

Kees-baboons — "Beast" baboons, horrible or nasty baboons.

Kerkplein — Church Square, often the central point in a town.

Kerkraad — Parish council of a Dutch Reformed church.

Klinkpenne — Joining pins, in woodwork.

Kloof — A narrow natural or man-made pass between mountains.

Konsistorie — Vestry.

Konventie — Convention.

Koppies — "Small heads", small hills, plural form of koppie.

Koster — The verger or caretaker of a Dutch Reformed church.

Kraal — A traditional African village, or an enclosure for livestock.

Landdrost — Magistrate.

Leegte — A low-lying plain or valley; a shallow dip or depression.

Leiklip — Slate.

Lekkerland — "Nice country," an expression of joy.

Likkewaan — A large monitor lizard.

Lowveld — The name given to two areas that lie at an elevation of between 500 and 2,000 feet (150 and 600 metres) above sea level.

Manel — A black frock-coat worn by elders and deacons of the Durch Reformed Church.

Mamba — A deadly snake,

Mealie — Maize.

Meneer — Sir, or Mister.

Mieliepap — Maize-meal porridge.

Miesies — A term of address to a white woman; also used in the third person, to show respect.

Morgen — A unit of land measurement comprising just over two acres, or one hectare.

Mshangaan — The Shangaan tribe, mainly living in the northern Transvaal.

Nagmaal — In the Dutch Reformed churches: the sacrament of Holy Communion.

Ouderling — An elder of the Dutch Reformed Church.

Oupa — Grandfather, grandpa; or a respectful form of address or reference for any elderly man.

Platteland — "Flat land," rural areas or country districts.

Plein — Square, as in a town square.

Poort — A narrow pass or defile through mountains, particularly one cut by a stream or river, also an element in place names.

Pouse — Pause.

Predikant — A minister of a Dutch Reformed church.

Prieel — Arbor.

Rant — A long (rocky) hillock; an area of high, sloping ground.

Ribbok — Small antelope.

Riempies — Leather thongs, often used to provide seating areas in a chair.

Rooi — Red.

Rusbank — A long wooden settle with back and seat made usually of woven leather thongs.

S.A.P. — South African Police, or, Suid-Afrikaanse Polisie.

Sechuana — The language of the Tswana people.

Simpel — Stupid, thick-headed; mentally retarded.

Sjambok — A heavy whip, formerly cut from rhinoceros or hippopotamus hide used for driving animals or administering punishment.

Spruit — A small stream or watercourse, usually containing little or no water except in the rainy season.

Stellaland Republic — An early independent Boer Republic, absorbed into the Transvaal Republic.

Stert-riem — A loin-cloth of soft leather, traditionally worn in rural society by Sotho men.

Stoep — Porch.

Tambotie — A deciduous tree with scented, durable wood and caustic sap.

Union — The Union of South Africa, the post-Second Boer War constitutional arrangement which saw the two former Boer Republics of the Transvaal and Orange Free State united with the British-ruled colonies of the Cape and Natal united under one government.

Veldkornet — A field cornet, an antiquated term used in South Africa for either a local government official or a military officer.

Veld-langers — Fortified places in the countryside, usually temporary.

Veldskoen — A shoe similar to a moccasin, made of rough (often untanned) hide stitched with leather thongs.

Vlakte — An open plain; an extent of flat country.

Voetsek — Go away, 'scram', 'get lost': a rough command, as spoken to a dog or (with either insulting or humorous intent) to a person.

Volkspele — Afrikaans folk-dances, created during the 1930s but usually performed in traditional Voortrekker dress.

Voorkamer — Front room of a house, also a reception room.

Voorlooper — The person (usually a young boy) who walks with the foremost pair of a team of draught oxen in order to guide them.

Voortrekker — A member of one of numerous groups of Dutch-speaking people who migrated by wagon from the Cape Colony into the interior from 1836 onwards, in order to live beyond the boundaries of British rule.

Vos — Pied, as in having two or more different colours.

Wag-'n-bietjie thorns — "Wait a minute" thorns. Any of numerous species of shrub having strong (usually curved) thorns, known as "wait a minute" because of their tendency to catch one unawares and delay passage while being unpicked.

Withaak — A thorn tree bearing hooked white thorns.

Witvoet — "White foot", as in "give gas" or "speed up."

Ystervark — A large rodent with a protective covering of sharply pointed quills which are banded in black and white.

CPSIA information can be obtained
at www.ICGtesting.com
Printed in the USA
BVHW050853080223
658122BV00007B/146

9 781647 644376